Kingdom of Magic

By
Leona Canry

Table of Contents

CHAPTER ONE

"Oh Kyle, I love you so much! I don't know what I'd ever do without you." Robbie laughingly teased, shaking her long, blonde, curls behind her shoulders.

"Robbie, please! You have no idea what you are talking about! This is not a laughing matter." Kyle firmly stated, placing his hands on his hips. "Can't you ever be serious?"-His green eyes stared at her, unmoving.

"I am serious." She tilted her head to look at him. "I'm as serious as a heart attack in the middle of a church service." She giggled while speaking. "I do love you," Robbie said, becoming more somber. "But marriage! It's a bit preposterous, don't you think?" She lifted her light sapphire eyes to his

face, after shaking her head.

Kyle shook his head. "No." He answered sincerely. "I wouldn't have asked if I did."

Robbie sighed. "Of course not. Why now of all times?" She asked. "Robbie, look around you. What do you see?" He responded. Robbie closed her eyes.-"We're on a sand dune in the middle of the Sahara." She joshed him again.

"Robbie!!" Kyle exclaimed, his emerald eyes widening out of proportion. He ran a hand through his thick, black hair.

"Well, we are on a hill." She pouted when she saw his glare. "Ok. You win." She looked around her. Green hills and grassy plains for miles, surrounded by blue and purple mountains, with clear skies. There was a rainbow to the east, and little white flowers blooming everywhere. It was truly breathtaking.

Kyle was growing impatient. "Well?"

"Well, what?" Robbie was lost in a daydream.

"What do you see?" He asked her again.

Robbie started rambling.- "A bunch of green flowery hills, some mountains, and... What was that look for?" Robbie asked Kyle, seeing his expression change from serious to pleasant.

"It's beautiful, isn't it?" He smiled. "Everything here is beautiful. That's why I brought you here." Kyle was still on his knees. He blew her a kiss. "Kyle!"

"Robbie, please. I'll give you time, if that's what you want," the six -foot-four giant plopped next to her.-He opened his hands, and cupped them together.-The middle of his palms was covered in rose petals. In the very center of the pedals, was a ring. "Please, Robbie." He paused and looked into her eyes. "Will you marry me?"

"What are you going to do?" Tinsa asked Robbie. Her other friends bobbed their heads, awaiting her answer. They had come in, unannounced, and uninvited. Word traveled fast in the small villages.

"Oh, I don't know guys." Robbie tucked a strand of blonde hair behind her ear. She looked around her room and saw everything that she had. She wasn't sure about moving away from her mother. She loved her space and free time. She sighed. "It's so confusing."

"Nelame, what did you do when Tenger asked you to marry him?" Latell asked her red-headed, dark-eyed friend, hoping that her answer would help. She popped a biscuit into her mouth.

Nelame laughed. "I'm not the one to ask! I'm such a bad example to ask advice for someone else's future." She shook her hair around, and then pushed it back behind her shoulders. "I was totally infatuated with Tenger. I knew what I wanted." She sent a side glance to her friend, and a sad smile toward Robbie. "Robbie doesn't know what she wants out of life."

They all looked at Robbie. "Yes, true." They all agreed. Carieve piped up. "Robbie, what do you want out of life?" She twisted her hair in her fingers. "I don't really know if the rest of us have a choice; Being women of our time." She nodded at Robbie. "You really got lucky here." She took a deep breath. "I hope that in the future women will have a right to choose what she does, if she

2

wants to marry or not." Carieve added thinking out loud. "How do you feel about Kyle?" She asked, adding to her ramble.

"Hmmmm. Those are great questions. Especially the former thousand, before you went on your rant!" Robbie answered, laughing. "I do love him. You all know that. I just don't know if I'm ready.... I mean look at me." She glanced down at her plain gown and bodice. "Then look at you!"

Carieve, with blonde hair a shade or two darker than Robbie's, blue eyes, so dark that they were almost black. She was very analytical; and tried to make the best of every situation. Sitting to her left was Tinsa. She was an exotic beauty. Long, black, straight hair shaped her almond face. Her silver-gray eyes were always empathetic and charming. Latell would almost be considered normal; if it weren't for her nature. She was always helping where she could. It didn't matter if it was a trapped squirrel; or an old lady. She had shoulder length, light brown hair and pale green eyes, framed with freckles.

"I mean your father's just ship you off like cattle to trade. Here I am, I do have a choice. And I am whining about it." Robbie stated. "I just don't think it's fair. I wish I'd had a father to make that choice for me. It would be a lot easier."

"Oh! Poor Robbie!" Tinsa exclaimed sarcastically. She then threw a pillow at her head. The girls' laughter enveloped the small cottage.

"Kyle, she had better say yes, or you are finished! You hear me, boy!" Movada demanded, sensing that he would not be pleased with this outcome. His fat face turned into a disgusting scowl. He was slouched in a chair, twice the size that he was, which was hard to find. He sucked back some mucous in his bulbous nose.

"Yes sir. I gave her a few days to think about it." Kyle responded naturally, not really caring. He feared for his life, and what this big man had to say, but he refused to show his emotion.

3

"Now wasn't that kind of you." He quipped, tilting his balding head. "I'll tell you one thing. That won't happen again." Movada took a stogie from his pocket and lit it. He rolled the cigar between his lips, as the juices from his breakfast came to play with it, around the corners of his mouth.

"What if she says "No." Sir?- What will we do then?" Kyle asked, raising his eyebrows.

"*We* will do nothing. *I* will come to that when I get there." Movada looked into Kyle's eyes. Seeing the resemblance of Kyle's father in them, he became irate. "Get out of here before I change my mind!" He shouted at him.

"Just promise me one thing, sir." Kyle stated. He stood straight, and thrust his hands into his pockets.

"And what's that? Kyle." Movada asked irritably, blowing out a puff of smoke in his direction.

"Promise me. That you won't hurt her. In any way." Kyle said earnestly. Movada shook his head in agreement, and waved Kyle out. Kyle walked outside.

No sooner than Kyle had been out the door, Movada turned to his henchman. His black eyes burned a hole into the man.-"Follow him. Don't let him out of your sight. In three days hence you are to report to me. I don't want to see you until then. If she says yes, fine. If she says no, kill him. Bring her to me." He took another puff from his cigar. "Do you understand?"

"Yes sir." Tivico answered. He nodded briefly, his blonde hair bouncing, as he ran to follow behind Kyle.

Movada sat and pondered on a plan. He laughed to himself. "I know I can trust them. They are too scared to do anything other than what I bid them."-He said aloud as his white Persian cat entered the room. Sydney sauntered slowly toward the throne-like chair. Movada picked up Sydney and methodically stroked his fur. Sydney purred and looked up at his master. "Is it right and good? You ask." Movada laughed at the cat. "My response to that is. I really don't care."

4

Kyle sat down at his kitchen table. He looked around his little, one-room, shack. He placed his elbows on the table and let his head fall into his hands. "What am I going to do?" Kyle thought. "If only my father were still alive. I wouldn't be in this mess in the first place." A tear slipped between his eyelids, leaving his emerald eyes wet and bloodshot. He raked a hand through his hair and stood.

"God momma, where are you? Were you killed in the dungeon like Father? Or just taken out to let rot somewhere inconceivable?" He thought for a moment. "I'll get it back! Don't you worry about that! The Kingdom will be back in our family's hands." He was strong and sure.- "Someday." He added solemnly. Kyle lifted his head and stared through the window with sightless eyes.

Tivico watched from a distance. "Poor bastard." He knew the feelings of someone who had been through a conscious hell. His blonde hair fluttered in the breeze, as he watched Kyle in his devastated mood. "I'd help you if I could. Same as I helped your father." He said to himself. "Unfortunately, I'm nothing more than a slave now." Tivico figured that it would do him no good to watch Kyle. Surely, he wasn't going anywhere in his current state of mind. Tivico found a spot in the hay to lay his head. His lean, muscular body was not hard to hide in the hay.

"You actually think that he will do it?" Shaddock asked with a laugh. "If I did, would I be talking to you?" Movada snapped. "Yes, or no, I want Kyle dead." Movada moved next to Shaddock. He grabbed his tunic in his fist and looked into his eyes. "Do you understand me?" He yelled. "All we need is a little Prince running around, getting married, and taking the Kingdom of Whispershire back to his family!" Movada released his hold. "No doubt causing trouble all over the place for me. Trying to kill ME in the same manner that I killed Rosseco." Movada's words rolled off his tongue like a snake's.

Shaddock nodded his head in agreement. "What about the girl?" He asked. He was thinking of taking Robbie for himself.

"We'll deal with that issue later. Right now, I have a job for you." Movada curbed his anger and became pleasant, all of a sudden. "It will require some traveling."-He smiled at his strongest, and most faithful henchman.

Shaddock stared ahead at first unblinkingly, as he thought of how to go about his new assignment. Slowly, he accepted it and went on his way.

"How do you feel, Robbie?" Clairance asked, gazing into a face that was much like her own. She came into the room and put down the basket full of eggs. Clairance took a seat next to Robbie, on her bed.

Robbie sighed. "I'm fine." She answered, rubbing her eyes. "What's the matter, dear?" Clairance asked. "And I'm not going to take I'm fine, for an answer. Not when you are rubbing your eyes like that!" She looked at her daughter and shook her head. "Please tell me. Did something happen this morning? With Kyle?" She pushed Robbie's hair back away from her face.

Robbie frowned at her mother. "No. Nothing like that." Robbie thought for a moment. Should she tell her mother? "Well, sort of... I don't know." Robbie sighed.

Clairance moved closer to Robbie and held her hand. "Tell me everything." She said looking at her.

"Well, we went horseback riding, way up into the countryside. The birds were singing, the bees were buzzing and you could still smell the freshness of the morning's first dew..." She trailed off as if in a daydream. After a few moments, Robbie turned and gazed into her mother's eyes. "He asked me to marry him, Momma."

"Then why are you depressed? Rob, you should be happy!" Clairance exclaimed.

6

"I don't know mother. I mean, he is the sweetest guy in the world. I love him to death, but marriage?" Robbie took a deep breath and blew it out with a sigh. "Is that what marriage is based on?" Her brows creased on her forehead.

"Honey, marriage is based on a whole lot less, sometimes." Clairance advised. "Kasde and I were married because it was a match made by the King." She looked at her daughter sympathetically. "Let me tell you it was quite the experience. We had never before, even laid eyes on each other, before the wedding.

"When I saw him, standing before the priest, with the King at his side, I was scared to death. I didn't know what kind of man he was, what kind of husband he would be, what kind of father. I knew nothing.

"Your father was a great man. He was an amazing husband. I got lucky. I did grow to love him. It is a pity that you didn't get to know him. I do not even know if he is still alive or not. Movada sent him away from me! From Us! He broke up our family. He threw the King and Queen into the dungeon with their son.

"Movada is a monster! He made the royals become personal salves." Clairance felt the need to give her daughter some more history. "Rosseco, the King, refused to work for Movada. He was whipped to death in front of his family. Zipurda cried for her husband; and did little else. She was tossed out, to beg in the streets. Movada told her that she was worthless. No one really knows what happened to their son." Clairance added. Except for me. She thought. "I think he was about two years older than you. Kyle's age I think." She hinted to her daughter to no avail.

"Ok, mom. What do you want?" Robbie was used to a history lesson followed by a chore of some sort. She figured that she might as well ask.

"Well, someone catches on quickly!" Clairance laughed and thought for a moment, about what she wanted from her daughter. "I want you to go into Camo Forest for three days. You will take nothing but a cloak, and a dagger. I want you to rely on your senses and the things that nature provides. Listen to your inner voice and all will be revealed in its due course." She looked at her daughter lovingly.

"That is my only advice for you. Now, you will leave on the morrow. As long as you do not leave the forest for three days, you will be safe. You will find out everything that you need to know." Clairance kissed Robbie on the forehead. "Take care, my daughter. You need to get some rest." Clairance stood and moved toward the door.

Robbie smiled at her mother and then remembered something. "Mom?"

"Yes, sweet-heart?" Clairance answered, turning back around.

"I told Kyle that I would give him an answer in three days." A frown creased her brow. "Wouldn't tomorrow be the second?"

Clairance patted Robbie's hand. "Listen to me, child. You must go into the forest before you talk to Kyle. You must engage the forest. You may not answer a question about marriage, without your father, unless you do this. Do you understand?" Clairance gazed into her daughter's eyes. "This is very important."

"But, Kyle?"

"In the morning. Leave. I will take care of everything." She cast her daughter a knowing glance. She shook her head and looked away. "I know Kyle will be worried. I will tell him that you have left and why, the morning after you have gone." Clairance reassured her. She patted her daughter's hand.

"Why tell him why, when I know not myself?" She asked with a laugh, getting confused at her own words.

"You are special. That is why. You were born into a family that has different traditions. That is all. I will tell him because he is special too. He needs to know. what you will soon find out." She was being vague and cryptic. "But you have to find out for yourself! I cannot tell you. That is why you have to go." Clairance nodded her head at Robbie and kissed her again. "Goodnight child. I will see you in a few days."

CHAPTER TWO

The next morning Robbie awoke early. She put on her cloak and grabbed her dagger. She pulled her long, blonde hair into a braided bun atop her head. She snatched an apple from a basket by the door, and walked outside.

"'Bout time you got up." Her mother said standing near the door. She had saddled and reigned a little mare, called Ablom. "Here's your horse. Don't get lost."

"I won't." She kissed her mother goodbye and climbed onto Ablom's back.

"Don't forget. Listen to your inner voice and all will be revealed." Her mother told her. Robbie turned her horse toward Camo Forest and speedily rode away.

"God, forbid anything bad happen." Clairance said under her breath with her eyes to the heavens. She went to the stables to continue the chores. She felt a tapping on her shoulder. She was startled. "Good heavens, you gave me a fright!"

"I am sorry Clairance. I heard you were sending Robbie back home. I thought I could catch a ride."

"Don't be silly Phoebe. You knew you couldn't." Clairance looked at her small friend. "Just think, when Robbie returns you may have a friend or two."

"Oh yes!! Finally! A new fairy! Do you think she will look like me? Oooh! Or maybe it will be a boy!" She squealed her excitement. "I've always wanted a family."

Clairance looks at her companion. Phoebe had been her companion ever since her mother had sent her to the forest. Phoebe had pastel purple skin, light blue eyes, and mint green hair. "It's been just us, for far too long." She responded, agreeing that Phoebe needed a partner of her own kind.

"Can I come with you today?" Phoebe asked. "I want to see the prince." She stood at her full height of four and a half inches. Clairance laughed. "I suppose. But you have to stay out of sight." She rolled her eyes.-"And quiet!" She added laughing at her little friend.

Tenger pushed his brown hair away from his face, to let more people see his newly grown, fu-man-chu. He was very proud of his facial stubble. He wanted everyone who saw him to know about it. His eyes were the darkest ebony. Many who were superstitious believed that he was a witch, because of them. Those same eyes were the main thing that attracted Nelame to him.

Both were quite young, around 20. They had been engaged for two months. They are still working out their differences. Tenger is extremely simple minded, and Nelame is almost always dead serious. At least that is how she likes to come across. Differences attract.

"Come on Nel, let's do something fun!" Tenger begged looking into her eyes.

"What, this isn't fun, just being with me?" Nelame stuck out her lip like a toddler pouting. Tenger came forward and nibbled at it until she sucked it back in. She smiled at him before becoming her serious self. "Can't you get a hold of yourself and your foolishness!" She scolded.

Tenger was stung by her smart retort. Instead of falling in line, like a gentleman would, he grabbed his groin; and fell to the ground. He rolled back and forth. "I'm trying, Nel! It won't stay still!"

Nelame tried to hold in her giggle. Expressing humor at such a thing was grotesque. "Tenger! You're such a goofball!" She sighed. "Tell me again, how much you love me?" She asked, glancing at him from under her long lashes.

He was completely still. He looked into her eyes. "I swear with all my heart, I love thee more than this world." He replied genuinely, laying on his stomach.

11

Nelame caught her breath. "I think you've bewitched me." She said sarcastically, implying the rumors.

"My love." Tenger sighed. He stood and placed his hand over his heart. "You won't be seeing any broomsticks under this bum." He moved next to her and pushed a stray hair behind her ear. "No matter what the town would say."

Nelame laughed. "Let's hope not." She said under her breath. She half hoped that he would hear her, and half regretted opening her mouth. Tenger caught her words. "Well, why not?"

She held her hand over her heart. "'Would damage my reputation!" She exclaimed.

"Is that all, Love?" Tenger moved away from her. "Is that why we are to be married? A silly reputation?" He rolled his eyes at her. "No." She replied. "I fear you would be hanged. Such things happen nowadays." Nelame smiled at Tenger's frown. "I finally have you thinking. Don't I?" She smirked at him.-"Tenger?"

"Yes, my love?"

"I do love you. You know that. I would not have agreed otherwise." Nelame moved closer to Tenger and kissed him on the cheek. "And no, it doesn't matter that my father made the match." She ran away from him. jumping onto her horse, she yelled "Catch me if you can!"

Clairance - determined not to ruin Robbie's relationship with Kyle, went to talk to him. "Kyle?"

She heard nothing. She knew he was there. "Kyle! Robbie needs a few days more to answer you!" She waited for a reply. She didn't receive one. One of the horses neighed and stomped its foot. "I know you are here. Robbie is out running an errand for me. She will be back in a few days."

Kyle sauntered out from the stalls. "Doing what?" He asked. "She went into Camo Forest."

"For what?" Kyle was confused.

"She is running an errand for me." Clairance repeated.

12

"When did she leave?" Kyle was exasperated. He shook his head, and looked as if he would throw up.

"This morning about five. She will return soon. Don't worry." Clairance told him. "Don't follow her either!" She warned shaking a finger at him. She was trying to be motherly. "As long as she stays in the forest, no harm will come to her. She has my specific instructions."

Kyle was irritably confused. He said nothing.

"Is there anything I can do for you today?" Clairance asked, smiling at him.

"No Clairance. Thank you for the information about Robbie. Now I have an errand that meets great haste. I have no further use for you at this time. Thank you for your willingness to help, and your generosity." Kyle smiled back for a moment then frowned. "I am sorry, but I do, bid you farewell."

"Very well, my Prince. I wish you the best of luck to you on your errand. I shall return to see you on the marrow." Clairance did a small curtsey and went home.

Kyle walked the pathway to the dreaded castle steps. He waited and stared at the castle walls. He was thinking of how to tell Movada that he needed more time.

Emilio came up behind him and grabbed him by the arm. "What are you doing here? Boy!"

"I came to see Movada. We have an arrangement." Kyle responded, jerking his arm back. "It's none of your business." He added.

"Then why haven't you been inside yet?" Emilio chuckled. "Your Highness?" He added sardonically. He popped his knuckles and grabbed Kyle again.

Kyle glared at him. "I can take my time if I choose." He responded. "Now remove your hands from me." He commanded.

"Well, now. The ever-haughty prince indeed!" Emilio laughed at him again. His large muscles flexed.

Kyle tore from his grip and took a step back. Emilio was prepared for this. A right hook caught Kyle near his temple. It left a bloody gash near his left eye. Kyle staggered backward. He wiped the blood from his face with his hand. Looking at it, he fell, unconscious.

"Not so high and mighty now, are you?" Emilio laughed. He threw the unconscious body over his shoulder. Emilio took Kyle down a long corridor to the last chamber. He pounded on the door with his fist.

"Who's there?" Warg yelled. "And stop your bloody pounding!" He swung the door open wide. His eyes bulged out from his face, as Emilio tossed Kyle to the floor.

"Here Nave! Take your boy!" Emilio laughed at the old man. He closed the door behind him. "I'll inform Movada that you have company."

"This place is so beautiful!" Robbie thought, coming to the edge of the forest. "What is this place?" She edged Ablom further into the trees. "Come on girl. We're almost there." She thought to herself for a moment. "I don't know how I know that. I just do. I can feel it."

Robbie saw a clearing ahead. She climbed off from Ablom's back. She glanced up at the sky. "I guess we will camp here for the night." She tied the reins to a tree, and removed the bit from Ablom's mouth. Robbie petted her horse, and ran her hands down her body. She heard a stream nearby.

Robbie followed the sound of the flowing water. She led her horse to it.They both drank thirstily. The water was cool and refreshing. Afterward, they felt revitalized and freshly awakened. Robbie decided that they should rest anyway. "Here is as good a place as any, Abby." She told her horse.

She set up camp in the middle of a grassy glade. She let Ablom wander to eat and drink as she pleased. Robbie meandered through some of the trees. She wanted to know why she was here. The scenery was beautiful. Everything was green. Nothing was dead or blemished in any way. Flowers seemed as though they had never seen a winter, and just kept blooming.

Robbie explored. She had a photographic memory. She wanted this place burned into her brain. She turned over rocks to see what type of insects were around. She didn't see any! She found some bigger rocks that she couldn't get to budge. She exhausted herself trying, then lay in the grass, pulling her cloak around her for the night.

Warg carefully squeezed cold water from a sponge onto Kyle's face. His wrinkled hands were sore from arthritis. He was about to give up on reviving him, when Kyle finally regained consciousness.

Kyle blinked. "Warg? Is that you?" He asked.

"Sure is." The old man nodded. "Been around you your whole life. I refuse to stand here and watch you die."

"You practically raised me." Kyle smiled at him and sat up.

"You raised yourself." Warg cut him off.-"I stayed put and watched. I won't forsake you." Warg smiled back.

"Forever thanks, Warg." Kyle looked around him. "How long have I been here?"

"Only a couple of hours." Warg scratched his beard. "I thought you weren't coming back for some time there." His eyes grew concerned. "What happened?"

Kyle looked at him and sighed. "Well, to make a long story short, I came to see Movada, and that ass wouldn't let me through."

"Well, you sure as hell found yourself in a pickle. I think you may have a concussion. You better get yourself home and get some food. Lord knows I don't have any here. You should be careful with that head." He continued to speak, walking back to his chair. "You'll have one hell of a headache for a while." Warg sat down. He looked at him sympathetically. "Lots of rest." He yawned. "And lots of water."-He nodded his head.

Kyle smiled at him and stood to go. "Thank you, Warg. I appreciate everything you have done for me. I will never forget you." Kyle left the old man to sleep in his chair. He closed the door quietly behind him and ascended the castle hall.

Shaddock rode Miduem long and hard into the next town, to deliver the message to the Duke of Vole Tirfs.

Remid ran to greet him. "Good sir, is there anything you require?   Shaddock leered at the servant from the house.

"You can tell the Duke that I have a message for him," his smirk broadened. "From Movada of Whispershire."

Remid recognized the name, and was no longer happy to be of service. He glared at Shaddock, his smile leaving his face. He ran to get the Duke.-"I beg your pardon, Sire. There is a man to see you." Remid knocked at the chamber door.

"Who is it?" The duke asked.

"I don't rightly know sire," Remid paused. He swallowed the bile in his throat. "He says he bears a message from Movada." The duke spat at the name. "Do you wish to hear it, Sir?"

"Tell him to meet me at the main gate. Let him go no further." The duke swung the doors open. He looked at Remid. "Take back up. He more than likely is armed, and is here to kill someone. "

"Sire?"

"Do it." The duke commanded. "I will take no chances with my staff." Remid retreated to the men's quarters to receive more guards. Shaddock sat on his horse and sneered at them. Movada had told him that they would be afraid. Three more men came near to him. "Go to the main gate and no further." The largest one said.

"And if I do?" Shaddock turned his scowl to him "Go further?" He raised a thick black eyebrow.

"You have your orders." Another guard said.

"Movada is my King! I owe nothing to your way lay duke!" He answered.

The duke entered the courtyard. "That may be true, but, Movada is no King." He glared up at Shaddock. "What is your message?" "Ah, Balcor! We meet again." Shaddock laughed at him.

"Get on with it, Shaddock!"

"You're mighty *testy* these days -since your brother died." Shaddock's eyes gleamed with his evil smirk.

"Speak your message or leave." Balcor commanded with vehemence.

"Very well." Shaddock smiled down at him from his horse. "Movada says that you have four days to swear allegiance to His Majesty. On the dawn of the fifth, if you have not, prepare to surrender all, or die like Rosseco."

"Do not use my brother's name!" Balcor yelled, ferociously. "Get off my land! I will never swear allegiance to that insolent, inadvertent vertebral! You may tell Movada that I, Balcor, Duke of Vole Tirfs, will never swear anything to him! We will never surrender!"

The courtyard yelled and hollered their approval. Shaddock turned his horse around and galloped away. In the distance, he could hear them shouting still. "Never!"

Tivico returned to Movada's castle on the third day. "Well?" Movada asked, seeing him enter. "What did the girl say?"

Tivico swallowed a lump in his throat. "I don't know Sir."

"What was that?" Movada demanded, daring him to say it again.

Tivico choked looking at the floor. "I do not know sir. "

"What do you mean you do not know?"

"I was watching Kyle like you said. He was depressed and talking to himself." Tivico babbled something incoherent.

"Get on with it!" Movada yelled impatiently.

17

"Clairance showed up. No one or nothing can hide from her. Kyle was talking to himself. They talked for a moment. It was brief. She left. I went back to where I was and Kyle was gone!" -He looked up.

"Damn it!!" Movada screamed and pounded his fist into his table. "How could you let this happen? You let him get away!" Movada stood. His face and eyes were red. "Get out! You are banished! I never want to see your sniveling, pasty face in this kingdom again!" He pointed to the door. "Get out!"

Tivico ran. He was not a coward, but he had to find Kyle.

CHAPTER THREE

Keesha looked at the ground and landed. Her little wings couldn't carry her that fast. She perched on a tree and looked around. She saw something shiny. "I wonder what that is." Keesha said, positioning herself to dive.

She lifted her little mint green arms above her head, wrapped her wings around her, and like a florescent pink torpedo, she launched. She landed gracefully upon a rock, using her wings to level her out. Coca laughed in the distance. Like a flash of light, the others joined her.

"Keesha, what are you doing way down there?" Tigli asked, blushing.

"Well," Keesha replied, watching them land, one by one. "I landed on that branch up there," She pointed to it. "Then, I was looking around. I looked at the ground, and I saw something shiny. So, I dived down here to find it. I just landed on this rock when I heard you laugh, Coca." Keesha explained.

"Dove." Strom corrected her.

"What?" They all looked at him.

"The word is dove. She was on the branch, and she dove." He explained, smoothing out his little white wings, with his little red hands.

"Like it matters, Strom. Don't be so uptight. She is the youngest!" Pixi exclaimed, stretching up to her full height of three and one-half inches.

"Yes, she is. And I am the oldest. Being ignorant will not help anyone's vocabulary-..._Dived is just wrong." Strom replied. Robbie thought that she was dreaming. She was hearing voices. They sounded to be right above her on the rock.

19

Robbie realized that she was awake. She moved slowly and sat up to peer over it. On the rock next to her, she saw seven little creatures. "Surely I am dreaming." She breathed, shaking her head.

The fairies shrieked as they became aware of Robbie watching them. Robbie soon realized that she wasn't dreaming; and that this was actually happening. She reached her hands toward the rock. Six of the seven jumped into her hands. The other stood back looking at her.

"Don't worry. I won't hurt you." Robbie licked her lips and offered her name. "I am Robbie. Who are you?"

"Pixi," she said. Then, she walked up Robbie's arm and stood on her shoulder. She took a strand of Robbie's hair that had come loose during the night, and picked through it in her hand.

"What are you doing?" Robbie laughed watching her with pure fascination.

"She's Pixi." Bo, a four-inch, black fairy with brown hair, gray eyes, and silver wings said.

"I see that. And who are you?" Robbie asked not sure what he meant. "Me? I'm Bo. But her, she's Pixi."

"What do you mean?" Robbie was confused. "I know she is a Pixi."

"You see," He tried again to explain. "She's not called Pixi 'cause it's pretty. "

"What Bo here is saying is that her name is Pixi, and she was given it for a reason. She likes to pick through things. She always has, and she always will." Strom interjected to help Robbie understand.

"So, who are the rest of you?" Robbie questioned. One by one they introduced themselves. The first of them was the tallest. He was a good six inches, with pale blue skin, silver hair, navy blue wings, and black eyes. This was Dery.

Strom had light red skin, bright golden hair, blue wings, and bright green eyes. He was five inches tall. Keesha had long fluorescent pink hair, mint green skin, misty purple, transparent wings, and bright blue eyes. She

was three and a half inches tall. Tigli had light gray skin, dark purple hair, blue wings, and bright green eyes. He was four inches tall. Pixi had light pink skin, dark green hair, violet eyes, and gray wings. She was three and a half inches tall. Coca had light purple skin, sky blue hair, gray eyes, and yellow wings.-She was four inches tall. "You are all so beautiful!" Robbie exclaimed. "Where do you all come from?"

"Behind the waterfall!" Tigli responded happily. He chuckled as the others "Shushed" him.

"No!" Strom yelled. It was too late. Now she knew their secret. "What?" Robbie asked.-"I won't say a word. Was he not supposed to tell me?" She sat up straight and looked at them.

"Villae will be very angry." Coca interrupted.

"Who's Villae?" Robbie asked curiously.

"She's an old witch." Bo said once again over-explaining.

"Just because she may be stern, does not mean that you should call her names." Robbie chided.

"No, no, no, no, no." Dery told her. "You see, she is the kind of witch that does magical spells, and has a crystal ball and potions and such." He explained.

"So, she is an actual witch?" Robbie was confused.

"Yes, but she is kind of mean, too." Keesha added. The others soon agreed, bobbing their heads.

Robbie thought for a moment. "Tell me," She inquired, "How is she mean?"

"Well," Pixi, using Robbie's hair as a rope to slide down to the others, said. "She locks us up at night in these big 'ol cages. It's dark and damp, and we're not allowed to talk to each other."

"Yeah," Coca added. "And the only way we get out - is when Kasde lets us."

21

That name sounded very familiar. "Who's Kasde?" Robbie asked, quietly.

"He's our caretaker." Dery answered. "Villae found him. He was passed out cold, here in this very spot!" He jumped down from her hands. He walked to where she was sleeping, and made an X with his feet, where her head had been.

"Hey!" Keesha exclaimed, once again her attention was diverted elsewhere. "What's the shiny thing you have?"

"Shiny thing?" Robbie asked.

"This." Keesha flew to Robbie's belt hook where her dagger was. She pulled it off from Robbie falling backwards.

"Give me that!" Robbie said. "It's bigger than you are!"

"What is it?" They asked in unison.

"It's my dagger." She told them.-"My mother told me to bring it." "What's a mother?" Coca asked.

Robbie looked at them. "She is the person who gave birth to me."

"What's birth?" Pixi asked. Picking at the dagger in her hand. Robbie was baffled. She didn't know what to say. They were like

small children.- "It's the human way of coming into the world." She said after thinking about it for a moment.

"Oh," They echoed.

"We must be going now." Coca said, noticing the sunset. "We told Kasde that we would only be out a little while."

"Yeah, we have been gone all day." Tigli added.

Robbie smiled as she watched them fly off. They looked like little fireworks shooting out into the sunset. They went further and further into a haze of bright purples and pinks, surrounded by the illusions that only the moon could portray in that instant. Robbie rose from the ground and went to find Ablom.

Kyle was in a daze. "How could so much happen in just two days?" He asked himself more than anyone else.

"Well, Kyle. You've had a lot happen to you, your whole life." Clairance answered, coming from nowhere. "Not to mention falling into the hands of an evil man. Don't you worry, your sweet little face. It is just the Fates playing with your head." She was concerned for the prince's future.

"Did you know that Movada is planning on moving against Balcor of Vole Tirfs? He tossed the question out, not really expecting a response.   "Good gracious! No!" She responded.

Kyle looked at her nonchalantly. "Pardon me for asking again, but are you sure, it's not too much to ask to stay with you; until Robbie returns?"

"Heaven's no. Kyle. It is a pleasure." Just then the door swung open, quickly. Clairance and Kyle stared at the open doorway.

Tivico stood breathless at the entrance. "Kyle!" He exclaimed. "Thank God I 've found you." Tivico caught his breath. "There is danger! Movada is sending someone to kill you! He'll kill Robbie too, if he finds her!" He was panting hard. He had run the whole way. He looked around the room looking for Robbie. Tivico panicked. "Where is she?"

Kyle vacated the chair he was sitting in. He grabbed Tivico by the shoulders. "What happened?" He demanded.

Tivico caught his breath. He looked Kyle in the eyes. "Movada sent me to follow you the last couple of days. He wanted me to tell him Robbie's answer before you could. He realized that if you get married, then you can take the throne. You would be the rightful heir. You could overthrow his ass!" Tivico stated.

"Hold on. Wait one minute." Clairance commanded. She looked at Kyle. "You mean to tell me that you asked for my daughter's hand to please that over-gratified oaf!"

"No, Clairance." Kyle answered. "You misunderstand. It's not like that!" He exclaimed, trying to redeem himself.

"I? I misunderstand?" Clairance asked. She raised a questioning brow. "Tell me, how?" She placed her hands on her hips.

"Clairance, you know me better than that." Kyle replied. He walked to her. He grabbed her by the hand, firmly, but gently. "You know I love Robbie." He squeezed her hand and let her go. "Please don't doubt my affection -or my sincerity. I would never do anything to hurt her in any way. If I did not feel this way, then I would not have asked." He reassured her. "No matter who asked me to."

Clairance flung her hands on the table and sat down harshly. "No. The point is, someone did ask. You did follow through. And 'twas for that conniving Movada nonetheless!" She argued.- "What about your family? What about your father? You saw him beat to death before your very eyes!" She shouted at him.

"Yes." Kyle firmly stated almost losing his temper.

"Do something about it!" Clairance demanded. She pounded her fists on the table.

"Pardon me for asking, but how much longer has Robbie gone away?" Tivico interrupted. He had been forgotten for a moment. "She may be in danger as we speak."

Clairance calmed and sighed. "She has another two days in Camo Forest. If anything goes to harm her, it shall not, as long as she stays in the forest. She is now under Villae's protection."

Kyle and Tivico exchanged confused glances. They did not know who, or what she was talking about. Clairance sat back down at her table. "My mother sent me there before I wed. Grandmother sent my mother before that, and so on and so forth. I'm passing along a family tradition." Clairance went into a trance-like state, remembering. "Kasde, what does she have you doing these days?" She wondered aloud.

"Was Robbie on horseback?" Kyle asked, trying to think of a strategic plan.

"Yes." Clairance snapped back to reality. "You mustn't interfere!" "Clairance, Robbie is in danger!" Kyle exclaimed.

"Yes, and it will be worse; if you so much as even breathe her way while she is in her passage! While she is in that forest she must hear, see, feel, only the things from within it. If something from the outside interferes, she will drop into a constant state of comatose, never to be heard from again!" Clairance looked at them strictly. She had never been crass with either of them before. "Do you understand me?"

Kyle and Tivico nodded. "Yes. We will not disturb her. What has to be, will be. I will not enter, but I will stop anyone else from entering it as well." Kyle said thinking that Shaddock may try.

"Never, huh? We'll see about that." Shaddock muttered to himself. He hit Miduem hard on his hind-quarters and yelled "I don't know why I put up with you beast!" He hit him again and dug in his spurs. "I said pick up the pace or be dog food! Don't you see the castle ahead?" Shaddock pulled the reins and Miduem stopped. "Stupid beast." He muttered.

Shaddock jumped off the horse. He looked at his front hooves to see if there was a problem. He found none. He then moved behind Miduem. He did not have any experience with animals. Miduem kicked him, hard, with his back legs. Shaddock flew back five feet. Miduem ran home, back to his stable.

Shaddock lay on the ground, stiff and sore. He thought about waiting for help. Shaddock thought better of it. He gradually worked his way to standing. He walked slowly, the half- mile to the castle. Once inside, he went straight to his chamber. He looked himself over for injury.

His strong, lean body, glistened with perspiration. He checked his flushed skin for cuts and infection. Bruises turned colors in prints of horse hooves on his finely muscled torso. Finding nothing else wrong, but his wounded pride, he went to his bedside and pulled out a finely bristled brush.

He brushed his long black hair into silken waves that fell just below his shoulder blades. Redressed in fresh clean clothes, he descended th hallway.

After knocking, the big oak door was opened to him, revealing a surprised Movada. "Shaddock my boy! You're back early!" Shaddock leaned against the wall and grimaced, as the words came out of his mouth. "The old buffoon says tell you, never." His words penetrated the air. Neither of them spoke.

Movada's grin turned into an evil scowl. His eyebrows arched inward. He held his lips tightly together; they were turning white from the pressure. The corners of his mouth turned up as he said. "If that's what he wants. So be it."

Shaddock's handsome features froze. "Sire, begging pardon for questioning your excellence, the townspeople are already in a saddened state. War would be less for them." Shaddock leaned forward, closer to Movada. He knew how to manipulate him. "And us. Do you really want to go without a meal?"

Shaddock looked around him. A long table beckoned forth the calling of servants. High-quality carved chairs surrounded the table. A throne made by the finest, for the rich was carved out of mahogany, with padded cushions for comfort, and decorated with jewels. Sapphires, emeralds,and diamonds adorn Movada's fat fingers. "Think of all we could lose for a mere five hundred sixty acres." Shaddock added pretentiously, thinking of all the material goods that he could lose if it came to war.

"Shaddock, my boy! You've got lots to learn!" Movada laughed. "Thinking of yourself never prevails." At least sometimes, he thought.-"Balcor will never fight. He is a coward." Movada smiled to himself. "Just like his brother."

Shaddock thought for a moment. He straightened. "What about Kyle? Is he a coward too? Most of the kingdom would rather follow him to hell than follow you to war. What of them?"

Movada laughed. "How naive you are! Let them be damned! I do not care!" Movada scowled at him. He laughed maniacally. "I took this Kingdom with a sweep of my hand. It shall remain that way. I will make sure of it, and so will you."

CHAPTER FOUR

"Tivico, I'm glad you've come to your senses. You're back on my side." Kyle told him, thinking that they would have to be friends to travel together.

"I am also, Kyle." The two men grasped each other's hands, briefly, as a show that they were in this together. They proceeded toward Balcor's castle.-"I am sorry if I took any advances toward you or yours. 'Twas to save my own skin!" Tivico stated.

"I know Tivico. I know you. You were scared to die. I can understand that, placing myself in your position." Kyle looked across at him. "I myself would rather die."

"And I can understand that, placing myself in your position, if I ever could. I couldn't, but I ask, if I could, I would be held in as high of esteem -as if your father were present?" -Tivico pleaded with him with his mannerisms. "That is if you would forgive me, my lord, if you would like to?" Tivico asked.

Kyle studied him from his horse. "How about we save my uncle -and my bride. We get the kingdom back; and avenge my family. Then you may be as whatever you wish." Kyle answered.

Remid ran outside the gates to greet them, as they neared. "Welcome young prince, Please, Balcor bids you and your guest come inside." He gave Tivico a quizzical look before turning back to Kyle.

"All in due time, Remind." Kyle told him. "Go and fetch my uncle. Tell him that I am waiting for him here."

"You're Highness. As you wish." Remid bowed and turned his retreat back to the castle.

Revie came from the West Cabins. He directed their horses to the stables. "Is there anything your horses require?" He asked. Kyle nodded. "Brush them down. Give them water and oats." He replied.

"Will that be all, Sir?"

"Yes, that will do. Thank you, Revie."

"Sounding more and more like your old man, every time I see you." Balcor said coming from behind them. "Kind-hearted and honorable, even amongst the servants."

"Hello uncle." Kyle embraced Balcor in a warm reuniting hug. "Been a long time." They stood back and admired one another. "You remember Tivico."

Balcor smiled at him as well. "How could I forget? One that serves well is oft times not forgotten."

"Thank you, my lord."- Tivico smiled back at him with acquiescence. "I hate to break this up and all, but the reason that we are here could be traumatic for us. If we don't get started."-He said as anguish crossed his features.

"Yes, yes." Balcor started stroking his beard. "What brings you to my door? And why won't you come in?"

"Uncle, we will sit in your study for a while. We have much to discuss." Kyle patted his uncle on the shoulder as they walked together. "Especially as of late." He muttered under his breath.

The men walked all together down the main hall. The study was next to the duke's chambers. Rich marble statues decorated their walkway. Stone gargoyles watched from above. Once inside the study, they entered a solitary room at the end. In the room, there was a large rosewood table. It had four chairs of the same delicate wood surrounding it. Balcor motioned for them to sit.

Kyle sat across from Tivico. Balcor sat at the end between them, looking out the door. A servant named Ganter brought in goblets and wine. He placed them on the table and left them to their business, closing the door behind him.

Balcor popped the wine cork from the bottle with his teeth and spat it across the room. He poured wine for them all. "Now, what is this matter that is so urgent?" He asked nonchalantly.

Kyle and Tivico looked at each other. Kyle stated "War." He swallowed a sip of the wine and then elaborated. "Movada is

29

planning a war. We, of course, are on your side. But, in return, I want your help. Uncle, you must help me avenge my father's murder." Kyle took another drink from his goblet and licked his lips. "We must show Movada how useless and powerless he really is.

"Tivico and I have spoken to the people of Whispershire. We have sent messages to all villages within 100 miles. All will go to war with Movada, bringing him here. Then they will turn against him at the last minute. You, or the people will capture him for me.-I will kill him. This gives me the crown, and our family back the castle and the lands. You win your war." He gulped down some more of the strawberry wine. "Is this acceptable to you?"

"Have you thought this through? I mean really thought it through, Kyle?" He glanced at his nephew and his servant. "Who is going to betray you and keep fighting? Who else wants the crown? Who is really on Movada's pay list? Maybe even consider, who wants to kill you?" Balcor paused for effect. "Have you made any enemies Kyle? I would seriously count them before a stunt like this." He eyed Kyle over his goblet. "Movada is smart. He is a force to be reckoned with."

"Hey girl. How are you doing today?" Robbie asked Ablom coming next to her. "Want to go meet my new friends?" She asked her. Ablom snorted in response. The more she thought about it, the more the names were familiar to her. Robbie absently led Ablom back to the rock where it had all happened.

"Let's see if we can find them." She climbed onto Ablom's back. Maybe if we find them then I'll find out who they are."-She led the horse in the direction they flew away to. "They said they are from behind a waterfall." She careened her hearing, everywhere around her, to locate the water where they had drunk from. "Maybe if we follow it back up, it will lead us to them." Robbie thought out loud. She followed the sound of water trickling on the rocks. She turned her thoughts into action. They were heading toward the strong currents.

Villae was watching her from her crystal ball. She threw her hands in the air and stomped her feet on the ground, jumping up and down. "Damn it! Sher's coming here! If only you hadn't let those blasted fairies out last night!" She thrust her hands into the pockets of her tattered and torn old cloak. She walked around her cave mumbling obscenities.

"If only you hadn't married my sister, then that meddling brat wouldn't be here!" Villae screamed.

"Calm down, Villae." Kasde told her. I for one would love to meet my daughter. He gave her a look of longing, that was so profound, she almost forgot what she was mad about. "Please, if you don't want to see her. Or in other words, don't want her to see you, then go and hide." His eyes filled with tears of happiness. "It's finally time for me to go home."

Robbie led Ablom across the meadow. She carefully climbed over some rocks. They didn't have to walk very far. She found it. "Hello?" Robbie called. "Is anyone here?" She climbed on top of the rock. She was next to the waterfall, but she couldn't see through it. Robbie leaned forward, and she slipped. Her face started to go toward the rocks. She screamed. Suddenly, two strong arms came forward and grabbed her. The next thing she knew, she was on the other side of the waterfall. She was only wet for a second. The arms released her, and she stood staring at a very handsome man. He stood about five foot eleven inches with graying brown hair and vibrant green eyes.

"Hi." He said. "I have been waiting for this moment for a very long time." He stretched his hand out and placed it on her shoulder.-"I am

Kasde." He smiled sweetly at her. He seemed so familiar. "Robbie, there is much to discuss before we go home tomorrow." He said ecstatically. At that moment Robbie remembered her mother's words. She opened her mouth but no words came to her. She stood there with her lips agape. "Yes, Robbie." He spoke. He smiled widely, but sympathetically. "I am your father." He knew how confused she must be. "I am the reason you were sent here." He heard a chirp in the background. "Well, one of them." Kasde was so overcome with emotion that he grabbed Robbie and hugged her tightly against him. "You were also sent here to bring back a mate for Phoebe." He released her.

Robbie took a step back. "Phoebe?"- Her brows creased and she shook her head. "Who's Phoebe?" Robbie looked around, very perplexed. "Oh, it never occurred to me that Clair wouldn't have shown her to you." Kasde raised an eyebrow and laughed. "She never told you about the fairies?"

Robbie shook her head. "Did she at least tell you that she used to live here?" He asked her.

Robbie shook her head again. "No." She replied. She looked at her father. He was a very comfortable person to be around. He wasn't too tall, or too thin. She could see the attraction her mother talked of. She tilted her head to one side. She wondered how she was at ease with all of this.

"She told me of your marriage, and how it was blessed by the King." She thought for a moment. "Mother said that I had to come here to consider my marriage." Robbie paused.

"To Kyle." Kasde finished for her. He took her by the hand and led her to the large table at the back of the room. There was a key pad where he pushed a sequence of buttons. A large crystal ball emerged from the center. Kasde put Robbie's hand on it.

The crystal ball started to glow. "I've been watching you, Robbie. I've been watching all of you." Kasde rephrased his words; because he thought that he came off a little bit creepy. "Clairance, my beautiful wife. Kyle." He paused for emphasis. "Everyone who is important to me. You."

Robbie jerked her hand away from the crystal ball. "But how can this be?" Robbie stepped away from her father. "This makes no sense to me! Mom said"

"Maybe I can help." Villae entered the room and cut her off. Her gray hair and black tattered cloak were flowing freely around her. She looked wild and inhuman. "I am a witch. I'm also your aunt. Your mother is Clairance. She is my sister. Our mother was a witch. I am a witch. Your mother is a witch and so are you!" She smiled weirdly and laughed. "Well, since your father is Kasde, you can be one if you want to." She corrected. Villae pulled a small bottle from her pocket and drank from it heavily.

Robbie was disgusted. She shook her head. "No. My mother said that I had to come here, to find the answers to my questions. Kyle asked me to marry him. That is why I am here!" Robbie looked at the smiles that crossed both of their faces. "Isn't it?"

The crystal ball grew brighter and brighter until the entire cave looked as if the sun was in it. When the brightness faded, Clairance was in the room. "Robbie, you already know your answer to Kyle." She walked over to her daughter and placed her hand on her cheek. "You love him. Don't you? I sent you here so I could have my life back." She looked longingly at her husband. "Phoebe also needed someone. I wanted to tell you desperately, but I couldn't."

Robbie looked at her puzzled. Again. "Why?"

"Rules are rules." Clairance shook her head. "This is the golden one." Robbie creased her eyebrows and stammered "To treat people how you want to be treated?"

"No," Clairance said laughingly. "I cannot show you until you have shown yourself."

"None of us could." Added Villae. She pranced around her cave. "And to tell you the truth I wanted nothing to do with this!" She looked at her sister and Kasde. "I told the two of you there would be nothing but trouble." She threw her hands in the air. "Argh... Mortals." She spit on the floor.

"What does all of this have to do with anything?" Robbie was growing agitated. "What does this mean for me?"

"Think, Robbie, Think." Villae came close to her and then backed up. "You could be more powerful than us all!" She said bitterly. Clairance rolled her eyes at her sister and embraced her husband. After a few moments, she turned to Robbie. "As long as you use the magic for the right reason."

Robbie huffed and thought.- "What magic do I have?" She asked, taking all of this new information in.

"You can do anything. As long as it is from the good of your heart, and it is to benefit others." Villae stuck her tongue out at her as if it made a bad taste in her mouth to say so. "Now come! We haven't much time. You'll find out soon enough. Let's go!" The four of them stood in a circle around the crystal ball. Clairance stuck her hand on it. Villae put her hand on top of Clairance's. Kasde reached out as well; and looked at his

daughter to do the same.- Their hands topped the other two. The crystal grew bright again. With a flash, they vanished with only Clairance knowing their destination.

CHAPTER FIVE

The door was opened to Balcor's chamber. The happy reunion of the family began. Balcor had invited the entire kingdom to celebrate the return of his nephew. Dancing gypsies were singing and playing fiddles. Fluttering their shawls like brightly colored butterflies, as they danced across the floor. Barrels of ale and rum were being carried into the dining hall; and emptied just as quickly.

The sounds of joyous laughter filled the rooms all the way down the corridor. The sounds only faded or dyed down some, when the boos were gone. - Large men fell to the floor in their drunken state.

"Have you chosen a wife?" Balcor asked Kyle. "If not then you have done yourself a favor coming to see me!" He laughed and pointed around the courtyard. "You may have any wench you desire."

Kyle watched his uncle's eyes dart around the room. "No thank you, Uncle, I have already chosen. She is making up her mind; if she wants to marry me, as we speak." Kyle answered honestly. "She is the only one I want."

Sariah placed her hand over her heart. "My goodness. Is it someone here at the castle?" She asked.

"No, Aunty. She is from my Kingdom. Her name is Robbie." The duchess smiled at him. The jewels from her fingers and neck were shining in the bright lantern light. "Sounds familiar. Is she by chance Kasde's daughter?"

Kyle was surprised. "Yes, actually. How could you have known that?" Kyle asked. He was becoming very apprehensive of attitudes toward him.

As of late his uncle yelled at him, and now they were acting like they didn't know Robbie. Sariah knew the family. Very well.

He wasn't the only one who noticed that they were being odd. Tivico was once again seated across from him. He was feeling very

35

uncomfortable, and showing it. He expected Kyle to make an excuse to leave. Kyle was trying to. Several times, he had said that they had other places to be. Sariah didn't want them to leave.

Kyle eyed them suspiciously. "We really must be going now. I am sorry uncle. It is imperative that we make good time." Kyle stood against the Duke and Duchess's protests. He shook and kissed each hand. He walked around to give his uncle a squeeze from behind and then kissed his aunt on the cheek. Kyle then bade them farewell, as did Tivico, which was expected.

Walking to the stables. Tivico and Kyle exchanged glances. They dared not speak lest they should be heard. Something was not right. They mounted their horses that were prepared for them. Once they had ridden a distance they stopped and looked back. "What on Earth do you suppose that was about?" Tivico asked.

Kyle glared at the castle. "I don't know, but I don't like it." He inched his horse forward, back toward the forest. Someone moved behind them. Kyle caught it in his line of sight. "Tivico don't look back, but we are being followed. Gradually edge the horse to go faster. You go left and I'll go right. We'll meet back in the middle, at the edge of the forest. If they are still behind us then we have no choice but to enter." Kyle took the reins and lifted them to him. "Go."

Each rider kept going faster and faster in different directions. Kyle and Tivico had planned it, but so had their attackers. Shaddock and Emilio came out from their hiding places and followed them, right at their heels. Shaddock rode after Kyle. He had things that Shaddock wanted; Robbie, and Whispershire.

Shaddock pushed his horse harder. His black hair came loose and flowed freely behind him. He pulled a bow and arrows from his back. His draw was around 50 pounds. He placed his arrow and aimed it above Kyle's back. He knew his pullback of estimated weight was correct; when he heard Kyle's tormented scream.

Up ahead, in the distance, there sounded a clashing of swords. Tivico and Emilio each fought for their lives. Against one another, their strength was equal. One trained to kill, the other to defend. Blood gushed from them both as the strikes landed on flesh.

Tivico lunged and tripped. Emilio's sword came through his stomach. He fell as though dead. Emilio came up to his body and kicked it. Tivico's form rolled over. As Emilio was seeing about his signs of life, Tivico's blade pierced him through the heart. Emlilo's shock shone on his features as he fell. He gasped and perished. Tivico was trapped under his large fame. He bled out, slowly and expired.

Movada's laughter filled Balcor's castle. He thought over Kyle's detailed plans that he had told him. Sitting there, listening like a trusted family member. He laughed again, loud and manically. The real Balcor would starve to death in the dungeon. Movada felt very proud of himself. He called for Ganter.

"Yes sir?" Ganter came forward. "What is it that ye be needing?" He forced himself to smile.

"Bring Sydney and I a large goblet of wine. Perhaps you would also like to join us as we celebrate?" Movada offered.

"Celebrate what, Sire?" Ganter loathed this. He scowled at the floor. "There is little to be thankful for."

Movada threw his hands down on the throne he was sitting on. "Ganter come and listen to a tale." He smiled mischievously. "See, I believe that there is much to be thankful for," he mocked. Sydney jumped into his lap. Movada scratched his cat's head, and he laughed sadistically. "See now, not only have I taken Vole Tirfs. I did it without a war, or warriors for that matter," he laughed again.

Movada tilted Ganter's head with the scepter; so that he could see the fear in his eyes. "And right now. Your beloved Prince Charming is probably bleeding out, or already dead." Movada smiled wide at the look of horror that crossed Ganter's face.

Ganter's eyes darted from each corner of the room. He stepped back from Movada's reach. "I'll get that wine now, m'lord." Ganter excused himself from the room. He became sick. He retreated more quickly to try and block out the sound of Movada's villainous laughter.

Kyle grunted and slowed his horse to almost a complete stop. The arrow that Shaddock shot was wedged in the back of his shoulder. He grimaced in pain as he reached to break it. He knew what he needed to do.

He jumped from the horse. Kyle found a tree large enough to hold his weight.

He clenched his hands into tight fists and rammed the back of his shoulder into the tree trunk. He shuttered in pain. He did it again, and again until the arrow- head pierced through him. Blood shot forward onto the ground. A tear came to his eye as he rammed it again. The arrow came though, enough to grab hold of. He reached up with his other hand and jerked it from his body. He looked at the tip that was used; and threw it to the ground. Kyle took off his shirt. He painfully tore a long piece from it. Kyle used it as a bandage and tourniquet. He breathed out raggedly and rested against the tree trunk.

"Well, you are the smart one, aren't you?" Shaddock said, coming upon him with his horse. "Too bad we aren't done yet." He taunted. Shaddock jumped from his horse and drew his sword. "Come on, Kyle. The fun is just beginning." Shaddock raised his sword above his head. He swung it around, showing his skill and the sharpened edge. Shaddock pointed it at Kyle. "It's just too bad that you won't be around long enough to partake."

Kyle saw the dagger in Shaddock's boot.- Shaddock's blade came for him and he ducked. He grabbed the knife, thrusting it upward into Shaddock's stomach. "Don't threaten me, you may not live to regret it." Kyle said as he twisted the knife before pulling it out again.

Shaddock brushed off Kyle easily. Kyle gritted his teeth and kicked Shaddock's legs out from under him. They wrestled for the sword. Shaddock gained hold and tried to stand. Kyle kicked it from his hands. Both men watched as it fell. Shaddock dove for it. He laughed out loud as the sword came back into his hands.

Kyle took the moment for a surprise attack. He jumped onto Shaddock's back. Shaddock spun around, trying to loosen Kyle's hold from his neck. Kyle let go with one hand, long enough to stab him between the shoulder blades. Kyle removed the dagger and went for his lungs and heart.

Blood spurted from Shaddock's mouth as he breathed in squeaks. "I always knew you were a back stabber," he murmured. Shaddock fell to his knees and then his head hit the ground. Kyle grimaced in pain and held onto his shoulder. He sat still, on the ground next to the dead man, trying to catch his breath.

Clairance landed them in a field, just outside of the forest. They heard the battles raging on both sides. Robbie watched as Shaddock fell. "Well, Robbie." Clairance looked at her daughter. "Now is your cue."

Robbie stood there and stared. She couldn't believe her eyes. "Well go on child! Heal him!" Villae shouted at her. "You know, as well as we do that you can."

Robbie ran to Kyle. Tears streamed down her face. "Kyle!" She shouted. She knelt next to him. Her hands knew what to do. One went to one side of his shoulder, the other to his other side. She looked to her mother and then to the heavens. Robbie took a deep breath. She could feel his pain as it entered her hands.

Robbie's body trembled. She closed her eyes and thought of healing. The bleeding stopped. Her hands dropped to the ground and she crawled to face him. "Oh Kyle, I love you so much, and my answer is yes." She kissed his cheek and unwound the shirt that he had placed. He tried to stop her for fear the bleeding wouldn't stop.

"Do you trust me?" She asked.

He looked into her eyes. "Yes." He whispered. She moved her hands methodically around the hole in his shoulder. She placed her hands on his skin where the blood had begun to stick. She let the magic leave her fingers and go into him. When she took her hands away, all that was left was a scar.

Her parents had come closer to watch. "We're so proud of you." Clairance said, helping Robbie up from the ground.

Kasde also helped Kyle up. "Unfortunately, we still have business to attend to." Kasde said. He looked to the other side of the field where Tivico and Emilio lay.

"You better start digging." Villae said. "I have my own business to attend to." She crossed her arms across her chest and vanished. Clairance wielded her magic to make holes in the earth for the bodies. Kasde shook his head at his sister-in-law's selfishness. He walked across the field to gather the bodies of the deceased. After Tivico, Emilio, and Shaddock were on the ground, they each grabbed one of the horses. "Something is amiss in Vole Trifs." Kyle told them about what had transpired there.- They rode together back to his uncle's castle.

No servants greeted them at the gate. Something was definitely wrong.- "Let's not go directly in," Kyle suggested. He looked around and saw no one. There had been a grand party earlier. "I'll go to the dungeon and start there. I'll work my way up. Robbie, go with your parents. I don't want to see you hurt."- He pulled her from the horse and hugged her tightly.

"I'll go with you." She laughed, and looked him in the eyes, "I don't want to see *you* hurt."

Clairance and Kasde laughed. They climbed down from their horses. Clairance grabbed all four reins. "We'll go in through the front door." Kyle shook his head, no. Clairance tied the horses to a pole. "I assure you we won't be recognized." She giggled as she waved her hands in front of her face. Her hair became long, red, and curly. She regained her youthfulness and her eyes went from blue to green. "Like?" She spun around for her husband's approval.

Kyle's mouth was agape. What was going on? Clairance did the same for Kasde. Even their clothing appeared to be regal and new. Kyle gasped. Robbie laughed again. "Just be careful alright." She hugged her mother first for a moment, and then her father for a moment longer. "I just got you back."

CHAPTER SIX

Kyle knew the place very well. Having been raised by Warg, they had come here a lot to visit his uncle. Kyle grabbed Robbie's hand and led her through a secret passage near the servant's quarters. Behind the gate; there was a latch, thought to belong to nothing. Kyle twisted and pulled it forward. The ground in front of them moved across, to reveal a spiraling stone stairway.

The staircase led into the lower dungeon.-"Stay close." Kyle whispered to Robbie. Still holding onto her hand, he descended the stairway with Robbie only a step behind.

"It's so dark," Robbie stated "And cold." She added. "There is no way there is anyone alive down here."

"Shh." Kyle told her, coming to the end of the stairs. There was a flickering light at the end. Kyle squinted to see what it went to. "Who goes there?" A weakened voice choked. "As the Duke of this, here, castle, I say," a cough erupted.-"Who goes there?" "Balcor?" Kyle questioned. "Where are you?" He quickened his pace.

"Go grab the candle and see for yourself. I am the only one down here."

"Uncle, it's me. It's Kyle, and Robbie too." He let go of Robbie's hand and grabbed the candle from its holder, on the wall. He flashed the candle into three or four cells; until he saw the light of his uncle's eyes flash back the flame. He grabbed the bars. It was locked tight. "Do you know where the keys are?" He asked, grabbing Balcor's hand.

Balcor coughed. "Over on the far wall." He answered. Balcor pointed to them with a long, bony finger.

Robbie grabbed his hands and tried to warm them. Kyle walked back to the staircase, and felt along the wall, using the candle for light. Kyle found them.

"How long have you been down here?" Robbie asked him, concerned. She took at his lean figure dressed in rags. "Poor man, how long has it been since you have eaten?"

Kyle unlocked the barred gate and it creaked open. Balcor looked at Robbie. "It's been a few days. Movada came and took everything over. Including my sweet wife. Movada came here yesterday. He said he would let me out. He grabbed my hand and changed. He turned into something else that looked and sounded like me." Balcor coughed again. His voice was weak. He struggled to regain his breath.

"Sariah was there with you. It was really her. You were our only hope. Movada laughed as he told me that you just left, against her protests to stay." Balcor grabbed Kyle's arm. "He said he had assassins waiting for you, and your friend. What happened Kyle? Where is your friend?"

Kyle led them back to the stairway with the candle. They stopped at the bottom. "We left here; because we had never been received so rudely by you before. We knew something was off. Sariah pretended to not know about Robbie." Kyle shook his head, remembering. "Movada did have assassins waiting." He swallowed. "Tivico is dead." Kyle answered.

The duke grabbed his arm with more force as he steadied himself to another coughing fit. "The assassins are also dead."-Kyle nodded to his uncle and patted his back.

"Can we please take this conversation to somewhere warmer?" Robbie asked, starting to climb the stairs.

Kyle smiled at his fiancé. "Yes, dear. But you're going the wrong way. We must get inside the castle. We need to find where everyone is." Kyle put his arms around his uncle and helped him walk. They turned to the right and under the alternative stairway. Robbie came to the other side of Balcor

to also give him aid. There was another stairway to ascend to the top. They made their way slowly out of the dungeon.

Clairance and Kasde paused near the front door. They knocked with the door hanger twice and waited. "I do not think anyone will answer."_ Kasde said, his voice suggesting that they break in.

"Me either, but if we are to be guests, then we must play the part." She smiled sweetly at him and kissed him on the lips, just as someone answered the door.

"Please, you must help us!" Kasde begged. "My wife is with child. She needs to rest and we have nowhere in particular to be." He bowed his head as he awaited an answer.

"Do come in, sir." Ganter replied. "I know not how the new master will take guests. I will be of any service you require." He led them to an empty servant's chamber. "Please stay as long as you wish."-He bowed and turned to leave. "I am sorry I cannot offer you more comfortable accommodations, at this time."

"Where is Balcor?" Clairance asked. "You said, new master? Where is Balcor?"

Ganter frowned. "He is in the dungeon. Movada is ruler here now." Ganter replied. He grimaced at the words. He turned and left them. Kasde closed the door quietly.

"Kasde we must go to him!" Clairance was frenzied with worry.

Kasde grabbed her shoulder and turned her to face him. "Calm down, Clair." He spoke. "Kyle and Robbie are already down there." He smiled into her face and pulled her in for another long embrace. "Besides, they may have already rescued him, and are probably bringing him to us."

"I suppose you are right." Clairance admitted, leaning into her husband, welcoming the feeling of his arms. She breathed him in and sighed. He kissed her mouth. "Well, I say we should adventure." She smiled at him. "Shall we explore the castle?"

Kasde laughed. "As you wish, M'lady."

"Oh, I haven't heard that in years!" Clairance exclaimed. They looped arms and began to wander the halls. Taking in the scenery as if they had never seen it before.

After retrieving the wine, Ganter obligingly entered the large room where Movada resided. Ganter handed him the goblet and sat the wine on the table, next to him. "Our vineyards' best." He bowed slightly. "And I am

pleased to inform you that we have guests." He blinked, waiting for a response.

Movada jeered at his mannerisms. "Since when do people drop by uninvited?" He chortled.

Ganter looked at Movada and smirked. "All the time. This is Vole Tirfs. When people need a place to stay, they know that they are welcome here." He replied.

"Is that so?" Movada sneered, with amusement. "So, is this generally a happy place?" He mocked.

"Yes sir." Ganter answered, glaring at him.

"Bring them to me." Movada commanded. He poured some wine and took a large gulp. He licked his lips. "I should like to see my "guests."" The last word rolled off his tongue like a snake's hiss.

Ganter swallowed the saliva forming in his throat. "Yes sir." He left to fetch them.

Villae was busying herself with cleaning her cave. She had no use for the things that Kasde accumulated over the years. She threw all of his things into a pile in the middle of the floor and set it ablaze. She organized her spell books in alphabetical order.

Villae had wanted her waterfall cave all to herself, since she was young. She reveled in it. She cast a spell that changed the location. She glared at the fairies. She unlocked their cages and told them all to "Get!" She tossed the cages into the waters below.

The fairies were free.

Exiting the room, Clairance and Kasde had come nearly face to face with a door that swung wide in front of them. They stood still as they heard labored breathing. Kyle, Robbie, and Balcor emerged from behind it, breathless and panting.

"Well, that was an easy find." Balcor laughed lightly.

"We were just coming to find you." Robbie added.

"We've just been accepted here as guests." Kasde told them. "Yes, and I'm with child and we have nowhere else to go." Clairance filled them in on the rest of the story. They looked at each other. Ganter came into sight. He saw Balcor, gave a slight bow and nodded. They retreated into the servant's chamber. Balcor, seated on the bed, waved Ganter forward.

"Where is Movada?" Kyle asked. "He's probably around here gloating and drinking himself into a stupor."

"Not quite but he is getting there." Ganter admitted. "He wants to see his new guests."

"How many is he expecting?" Balcor asked, catching his breath. Clairance and Robbie went to his sides. They sat next to him and placed their hands on his arms. They looked into each other's eyes and nodded. They pushed magic into his veins. His color came back to his face. His eyes brightened.

Ganter smiled at them. He fetched some water and bread from the hall. Balcor ate it savagely. "Just two, My Lord." He answered his question, finally.

Ganter led Clairance and Kasde in their changed forms to Movada's chamber. He had drunk half of the bottle of spirits that Ganter had brought to him only a few minutes earlier.

"Come on in. Do not be shy." Movada commanded them. "Do come closer. Let me see who you are."

Clairance bowed slightly. "I am Anitta LeBarron, and this is my husband, Marc." She spoke.

Movada smiled at her lop-sided. "How long do you plan on being with us?" Movada's eyes ran over Clairance. He was full of lust. "Your beauty has not been surpassed." She shivered from his gaze. "I shall require, no, no I shall insist, that you accompany me tonight in my bedchamber."

Clairance's stomach lurched. "You forget, *kind sir*, that my wife is with child." Kasde declared, glaring at him.

"Care ye not to share such a rare possession with your King? Movada carelessly baited him. The wine was affecting his judgment and loosening his tongue.

Kasde's hatred for the man grew in his chest.

"Maybe you should not see her again," Movada moved from his throne. "Would that be better? I could send your bastard away, and have my way with her, every night." His drunken laughter filled the castle. He moved to stand next to Clairance. He breathed in her scent. He reached for her. She whimpered. She moved away quickly, darting from his reach. Movada fell.

Movada glared at her, from the floor, slobber dripping from his lips. He stayed down, laughing at them.

"Robbie, I have to." Kyle told her desperately. "Now is my chance." He turned his attention to the room where the laughter was coming from. He turned toward the door.

"Kyle! Wait!" Robbie cried. He turned back to her. He stormed across the room and kissed her hard, on the mouth. He released her. "Please, be careful." She pleaded. She snapped her fingers in the air, and rope appeared in her hands. "Bind him with these. I'll be along in a moment."

Balcor stared at the girl who was to become his niece. "Robbie, be careful. You have a good thing going for you. You will soon be a Queen."

"Balcor, riches are not what I seek." Robbie shook her head at him. "A family is all that I need." She smiled sweetly. "Is there another way into that room?"

47

"There is a side door that comes in from the kitchen." Balcor asked "Why?" inquisitively.

"Just in case."

"Get up! You drunken fool!" Kyle commanded Movada. "You stole everything from me! Everything I ever had! Every dream that I ever dreamed! You destroyed it! You had to have your filthy hands in everything! You made me a servant! You killed my father! You threw my mother to the four winds!" Kyle choked on his words. His throat tightened. He swallowed. "It's time for a taste of your own medicine." Kyle walked closer to him and yanked him to his feet by his hair. "You hear me! Movada!" Kyle screamed. "I said stand!" A tear ran down his face. Every memory that came back to him from his childhood tugged at his emotions. He saw this man whipping the life from his father, and laughing at every lash that made his father scream out in pain.

"It'll do you no good, Kyle. Every effort on this man is to no avail." Ganter smiled and whispered. "I poisoned the wine."- He bowed his head. "Do with me what you will." He swallowed. "I am not sorry."

Kyle saw Ganter through veiled eyes. He cleared his throat. "Head up Ganter." Kyle sighed. "You have done well. I believe that we have acted rashly under the circumstances." Kyle walked to the wine bottle and crushed it over Movada's skull. He wanted to feel something to get rid of his inner torment.- He stood over Movada's body staring down at it in disgust.

Balcor joined them in the room. He placed his hand on Kyle's shoulder. He massaged it gently. "There is nothing that can be done, now son."

Kyle stood. His eyes were glassy from the tears that he had shed. He looked at his uncle. "There is plenty to do. I am twenty-two years old. I will run my kingdom the way that my father would have." He breathed heavily and left the room.

Clairance shed her magic spell and transformed back into herself. She watched Kyle leave with a heavy heart. Robbie looked at them all baffled. She was silent. Reality struck her. Kyle was the little Prince her mother had told her about. She shook her head.

Clairance moved toward the door. "I should go talk to him."

Robbie breathed. "Mom! Stop!" Robbie looked into her mother's eyes. She searched for all of the truths that she had missed.

"What is it?" Clairance asked her daughter.

"I think that I should talk to him first." Robbie smiled trying to convince herself of it. She found Kyle outside staring at the sky. She quietly sat next to him. "Kyle?"

He didn't answer or look at her. "Are you ok?" She placed her hand on his shoulder. She wasn't sure what to say. Her mind was racing. Yesterday she didn't know she could wield magic, she didn't know that Kyle was a prince, The Prince. She had learned that her father was alive, and she had a crazy aunt. She had met fairies! She stared at the sky with him.

"I don't see how so much could happen in so short a time." Kyle said before looking at her. He gazed into her eyes. "I feel like my entire life has just been a game, a set up," he paused and shook his head, "a mistake." He lowered his gaze.

Robbie careened her neck.- "You feel that way about everything?" Robbie asked him.

Kyle reached out and stroked her unbound hair. "No." He smiled sadly, at her. "Not everything." He grabbed her hand and brought it softly to his lips. The gentleness in his eyes startled her. She had never seen this look from him before. Contrasting with his shaggy, black hair, his green eyes were so light that they were almost gray. "I love you, Robbie." He said, "I don't ever want to lose you."

Robbie smiled at him. She could feel herself drifting further into a fantasy world, where only she and Kyle existed. "I love you too." She said quietly. Robbie closed her eyes and leaned into his strong frame.- His embrace is where she always wanted to be. Forever.

CHAPTER SEVEN

Back in Whispershire, it was a happy day. The reign of tyranny was over. On December 21, the entire kingdom was invited to crown their new King. Kyle stood with the people. He walked gallantly up the red carpet that had been thrown before him.- The people cheered.

Balcor and the high priest waited on the top steps of the chapel. Kyle strolled toward them. Balcor had Rosecco's crown. It was polished and ready for his son to take his place. The priest waved his hands. The crowd became quiet.-"Kyle, son of King Rosecco, and Queen Zipurda," the priest apportioned the passing of the torch, loudly to the crowd. "You are the rightful ruler of Whispershire." He handed Kyle a scepter. "Do you swear an oath to protect your people, to respect their wishes, to rule with honor, and to judge them according to the laws that have been pronounced before you?"

"I solemnly swear so to do." Kyle answered. He knelt before his uncle and the high priest. The priest put an anointing oil on his head and said his prayer in Latin. Balcor readied the crown. He placed it on Kyle's head when the priest had finished.

"Rise, King Kyle, and face your people."

Kyle arose slowly. His crown shined brightly, made of gold and rubies. His cloak was of Royal purple with golden trim. He wore a white tunic and black breeches. His black boots were also clean and shiny. He looked out over the crowd.

They cheered loudly for him. Some threw flowers at his feet. His people needed a new kind of ruler. They were peasants, poor, and hungry. Their clothes were clean for the outcoming; but still were completely worn. He could see the black rings under all of their eyes. They had toiled and worked their fingers to the bone. They had been no more than slaves here.

"For the past 15 years," Kyle spoke. "There has been no good among us. We have all worked and slaved for a tyrant! He has taken many things from all of us. Now, he is dead!"

The people shouted and cheered.

"I will rule justly, like my father did. I will repay what has been stolen from you. I will work, and toil with you to rebuild this once-great kingdom. We, together, will make Whispershire, all that it should be."

He watched for Robbie and her family. He met their eyes. Kyle nodded to them. "My first act as King is to appoint royal advisors. Kasde and Clairance helped me when no one else would. They helped me in my fight against Movada. They also helped me rescue my uncle when he tried to take his kingdom away."

"Here, here!" Balcor shouted.

"I insist that they move their family into the castle, immediately." He nodded to them again. Clairance and Kasde smiled and nodded their agreement. "I also will take a bride," Kyle continued.

Some of the young women of the kingdom gathered with bright eyes, smiling at him. He acknowledged them and then turned to Robbie. "If she will have me, Robbie, will you marry me?"

Kyle opened his hand for her to join him. She smiled wickedly and accepted.

"I cannot have the betrothed living in the same household. It is a sin." The priest advised.

Robbie and Kyle looked at each other. "I could stay at the farm, until we are ready." She told him.

"Nonsense." Kyle replied to her. He smiled at his uncle and then at the priest. "If you don't mind Father," Kyle started, getting louder he yelled, "Marry us then, everyone is already here."

The crowd erupted in cheers. The single young ladies cried at missing their chance. Kyle had been a friend to them all. Clairance and Kasde joined their daughter on the church steps.

The priest nodded, and smiled his approval. "Are there any objections?" He searched the crowd. No one said a word. All smiles as far as the eye could see. The priest sighed.

"Robbie, would you come forward please." The priest beckoned her. Balcor moved to stand at Kyle's side, as did Warg coming from the building. "If all is as it should be," the priest looked at them and they nodded.

"Kyle, take Robbie by the right hand, with yours." The priest instructed, "Now face each other."

Kyle looked into Robbie's eyes. They were both smiling. Robbie was wearing a blue velvet Victorian-style gown. It suited their purpose well. The color of the gown made her eyes even more blue. She had twisted knots on her head at two places in the back. Her hair cascaded from them down her back in blonde waves.

"Do you Kyle, take Robbie, to be your lawfully wedded wife, to love and to cherish, in sickness and in health, in joy and in sorrow, in pain and in bliss, for as long as you both shall live?" The priest looked at him for his answer.

He stared into Robbie's eyes as he said "I do."

"Do you Robbie, take Kyle, to be your lawfully wedded husband, to love and to cherish, in sickness and in health, in joy and in sorrow, in pain and in bliss, for as long as you both shall live?" The priest turned his attention to Robbie.

She continued to stare into Kyle's eyes as she said "I do." The priest nodded his approval. "Turn and face your crowd. Raise your joined hands." Asthey did so, the crowd cheered.-"I now pronounce you, in front of all of these witnesses, to be man and wife. You may now kiss your bride."

Kyle and Robbie brought their hands down from the sky and wrapped them around each other. Their heads tilted ever so slightly. Their kiss was pure and unhurried. They smiled up at each other. And faced the crowd again, to the "whooping and hollering."

A servant girl came forward with another crown of gold and jewels. She handed it to the priest with a bow; and disappeared into the crowd. "Robbie, step forward."-The priest told her. He handed her the scepter. "Do you swear an oath to protect your people, to respect their wishes, to rule with honor, and to judge them according to the laws that have been pronounced before you?"

Robbie licked her lips. "I solemnly swear so to do."

The priest nodded. He anointed her head with the holy oil and placed the crown on her head. "Then rise, Queen Robbie!"

She turned and faced the people. They cheered and threw more flowers. Robbie bowed to them and then to her King.

Balcor raised his hands to the sky. "I give you, people of Whispershire, your King and Queen!" He yelled. The people yelled back and cheered until they no longer had voices. "Come feast with us. We have prepared plenty!" Balcor told them all.

Music started in the square and the people started dancing in the street. Kyle and his new bride joined them. Later that day they sat at a

grand table. Kyle was still uneasy. He needed to know for sure what happened to his mother. He felt that Movada deserved more punishment. He should have been tortured. He got out too easily. He needed to find his mother. At that moment he thought of something. "Warg will know!"

"What?" Robbie was confused at his sudden outburst. "Warg will know what?"

"Where to find my mother." Kyle told her excitedly. He grabbed her hand and led her into the castle. Warg had never left. He was tired from the ceremonies; and had gone back to his room to lie down. "Warg!" Kyle exclaimed, entering his chamber.

"M'Lord." Warg addressed them, "What brings you here?"
"Well," Kyle started, "This has been bothering me for a while. I don't know for sure what happened to my mother. I was young. I don't remember all of the details."

Warg's smile lessened. He looked at Kyle sympathetically. "Oh. Your father was beaten to death by that awful creature, then your mother was tossed into the streets." Warg scratched his head. "Things are hard now.-I don't know what he wanted with you, but obviously, it didn't work." He shook his head. Warg took a deep breath and let it out slowly. "Your mother fell sick. She died of Pneumonia, some time ago." Warg squeezed Kyle's hand. "I'm very sorry."

Kyle didn't know what to say. He just stood there.

"Is there anything else I can assist you with, my grace?" Warg asked.

"No." Kyle stated. "Thank you. That'll be all." Kyle stood still a moment longer taking it all in, before retreating back up the corridor. "Are you ok?" Robbie asked him. She was very concerned. With everything that had happened since they came back from Vole Tirfs, he had been kind of distant.

Kyle didn't answer right away. He sucked a breath in through his teeth. His eyes darted around the room where they had stopped. "Yeah," he breathed out. "I just thought I could fix it." He looked into her eyes. "I thought that I could find my mother and bring her home." His voice cracked. "I just wanted to have my family together, like yours."

"Oh, Kyle." Robbie shook her head as a frown creased her brow. "Greetings my King and Queen." Ganter said as he waltzed into the room, unannounced. "Balcor begs of you to return to your feast." He wiggled his eyebrows at them. "Your celebration! Your new life, and new bride!"

Kyle looked surprised. "Tell him," He paused, not knowing exactly what to tell him. "That he is welcome anytime and may eat as he sees fit."

Ganter laughed. "He also said to give you this." Ganter pulled a present from behind his back. He handed it to Kyle. Kyle smiled and gave Ganter a look of bewilderment. Ganter watched their eyes light up at the sight of a stuffed cat, which they pulled from a bag. Ganter laughed again. "It was Movada's. Balcor said that it was as evil as he was."

Kyle laughed. He shook his head and handed it to Robbie. "I see." Kyle thought for a moment. He removed the furry thing from his wife's hands and handed it back to Ganter. "Go to the village and give it to Tinsa. You will find her selling corn."

Ganter looked at him perplexed. "Excuse me, sire?"

Robbie laughed. "Give it to Tinsa, and if you are crafty enough about the approach, you might also find a woman to woo!"

Kyle laughed. With Ganter's look of surprise, Kyle added "That's an order."

Robbie giggled a little, standing next to her husband. She turned and kissed him. "You are too much." She kissed him again and laughed at his expression.

"Not sure about that. Are you hungry? Shall we feast?" Kyle asked her. He kissed her cheek and then whispered in her ear "Or shall we conclude our wedding night?"

Robbie blushed. They had been flirting away, pining for one another for years. What was once innocent had become their life. She leaned into him and kissed him passionately. That was all the answer that he needed. Ganter left them. Kyle led Robbie upstairs. The royal chamber awaited

them. The bedroom was huge. There were deep red tapestries hung over the windows. Gossamer billows of silk hung from the bed posts. Dressers made of the finest mahogany adorned the walls. There was a large metal tub to the right and a walk-in closet.

Robbie had never been in this room before. She caught her breath. There was also a vanity and a couch, along with a rocking chair and ottoman of the same color.- The bedspread was handmade. Kyle rolled it down to reveal white, satin sheets. He sat on the bed and beckoned for her to come nearer.

"My love, you do not have to do anything that you don't want to." He told her, taking in her look of shock, as fear of what may come between them.-He took her hand to his lips, kissing it softly.

Robbie looked down at him. Her hair came forward and brushed against his face. She chuckled. She placed his face in her hands and looked into his eyes. "I love you." She kissed him on the forehead. She licked her lips. "I am not afraid of you. I have never seen so much wealth and comfortable things in one place." She chuckled again, glancing around the room.

Kyle smiled. "You will get used to it." He stood and walked to a dresser. From the top drawer he pulled out a diamond ring. He walked back to Robbie and took her hand. "My wife." He said as he slipped it onto her hand.

Robbie gasped as she stared at her finger, now adorned with the jewel. A tear came to her eyes. "It's beautiful!" She exclaimed. He kissed her on the lips. "You are beautiful." He told her, smoothing her face with his hand, wiping away the tears that had fallen. "Together we will do many great things." He sat on the bed again. He pulled off his boots and socks before laying back. Kyle sighed as his head hit the soft pillows. "Come and lay with me."

Ganter made it to the village. He spotted the barrels of corn. The girl nearest to them was gorgeous. Long, beautiful, black hair surrounded her almond-shaped face. "Excuse me, are you Tinsa?" Ganter asked, clearing his throat.

She looked up from her labor of shucking and husking corn. For one quick second, her silver-gray eyes met with his baby-blue ones. She began hanging corn to dry and grinding dried ones into flour. "Yes." She said.

Ganter was mesmerized by her. "You have a delivery." He said after swallowing the lump forming in his throat. He held the cat out to her. "I believe his name was Sydney." He spoke.

"Oh. A present for me? Who from?" She asked. She smiled at him and reached for it. Ganter wasn't sure whose name to say, his, Kyle's or Balcor's?

Tinsa laughed at the confusion that crossed his face. "What is your name?" She asked him.

Ganter laughed. "I'm Ganter." He stammered out. "I'm sorry love, but you are so beautiful, I was mesmerized and couldn't speak." Tinsa smiled at his remark. "Wow!" She moved her hair from off of her shoulders. "So, who sent you, Ganter?" She asked again. His expression revealed everything. "I noticed the hesitation when I asked you who you were."-She added.

Ganter laughed. "I was sent by Kyle."

Tinsa creased her brow and made a crooked smile. "My best friend Robbie's new husband, King of Whispershire, Kyle?"

"Yep. That one."

Tinsa frowned for a moment. "Why would he send me a stuffed cat?" She tossed it into one of her baskets.

"I really don't know." Ganter replied, completely stricken with her. "You know," Tinsa said, looking at him. "You're cute. We should go for a walk later."

Ganter was dumbfounded by her boldness. He did not know what to think. He had never met a girl so pert. "Yeah," he said. "I'd like that." He smiled unabashedly at her. "When do you get off from your shift?"

"Now.' She said. Tinsa took off the apron and flung it over a wooden box cart. "Ready for that walk?" She looked into his eyes and sauntered, sexily toward him.

Ganter licked his lips. "Absolutely. Where would you like to go? He asked him quizzically.

She shrugged her shoulders. She laced her arm in his. "Anywhere." They walked arm in arm around the village. Tinsa was informing him of everything that was readily available in their market, as they passed the work-stations. Ganter smiled at her and just listened to the tone of her voice.

Villae watched all of this from inside of her cave. Through her crystal ball. She could see anything. She watched civilization and she kind of missed it. She had always had someone here to talk to. Even if she had never wanted to. Ever since Robbie was born. Kasde was her companion.

She hated to admit it, but she kind of missed him too. The way that he had with fairies was amazing. "Well," she thought, "aren't they celebrating my niece?" She laughed out loud. "That would be perfect!"

Villae ran around her cave. She threw some of this and some of that into a huge cauldron. She tilted it from side to side and made it spin. The cauldron shook as she spoke her spell. It cracked and shattered into a million tiny little pieces.-Villae shook her fingers at it and snapped. The cauldron went back to normal.

When she lifted the lid, its contents turned into a lovely sapphire-colored dress, with a raised red corset. "Perfect!" She exclaimed, going over to it. With another snap of her fingers. It was on her body. She tilted her head and said another incantation. Now, she was on her way to Whispershire.

"Oh, what a month!" Clairance sighed. She was finally able to relax. They had just moved into the castle; and unfinished packing. "Now everything is as it should be. I have my husband, Robbie, and Kyle. Even Phoebe is happy here."

"It is so great to be home." Kasde agreed.-"I have missed you so."

"And I you." Clairance looked at Kasde with tilted eyes and blew him a kiss. It was just too much, to move back across the room for a real kiss, after moving.

Phoebe and Dery flew in through the open window, holding hands. They landed on Kasde's lap. "Thank you so much for uniting us as companions." Phoebe smiled at him.

"This is great. Thank you." Dery agreed.

"It is so good to have you with us." Clairance told him. "It's been a while for Phoebe and I. All of this secrecy was almost unbearable." "For you and me both, sister." Phoebe added. They all laughed and decided to get out a puzzle.

Setting up on a coffee table in the middle of the room, they heard a buzzing sound. Fast wingbeats that could only be a fairy. Suddenly they landed on the windowsill. All six fairies had found them.

CHAPTER EIGHT

Ganter was having the time of his life. So was Tinsa. She had never met someone like him before. Nor he, with her. In fact, he had told her so, many times, on the chance that they were together.

"There will be a grand celebration at the castle in a couple of days. Will you do me the great honor of accompanying me?" he asked her. Tinsa laughed. "There is?" She asked with mock humor. She winked at him and smiled. "I have heard rumors of it. Yes. I would love to." They walked along the stream, and back to the village, where he had first met her.

"Well, I have to get back and tell the duke the same thing." Ganter smiled at her. "I hate to go." He leaned down to kiss her, "But I have to." She resisted and pulled away.

"I'm sorry. The time is not right." Tinsa thought for a moment. "Do you by chance have other people coming? You know from Vole Tirfs?" She asked, rubbing her chin with her forefinger and thumb.

"Yes, of course." He replied.-"Why?"

"Well see, there is more than just me that's single around here. There are two more girls my age. Also, they are Robbie's friends. If I get to go then they should get to go too!" her expression changed. "Of course, they will need escorts." She smiled at Ganter.

"Oh, I think I know the perfect two." Ganter agreed, shaking his head. "I'm sure I can arrange something." He thought of the servants who did not have wives. He smiled. "Revie and Remid. They are my fellow associates in the service of our Lord, the Duke, Balcor."

"Revie and Remid?" She asked.-"Ok. Let them know that they are now taken." She stuck her tongue between her teeth, as she smiled at him, half laughing.

"What are the names of your friends?" Ganter asked. "I may need to know, to let my lord know, of our doings."

Tinsa smirked at him. "Latell and Carieve." Tinsa thought for a moment and smiled wide. "Trust your friends to my friends?" She asked. "Of course." Ganter laughed.-He winked at her. "Especially since the King did." Ganter laughed again. He wiggled his eyebrows at her. "We shall both have to thank him."

She nodded her head in agreement. "You're right. We will." Tinsa said, thinking of doing exactly that. Ganter set on his way to Vole Tirfs and Tinsa walked to the castle.

"Kyle!" She yelled. "Robbie!" Tinsa yelled even louder. She wanted to make them come outside. "Good evening, your majesties." She smirked as she said it; when they were within hearing range.

"What on Earth?" Robbie asked her.

"Well. I just wanted you to know that I've had a busy day." Tinsa laughed at their look of shock.

"Tinsa what are you hiding?" Robbie asked, a frown creasing her brow.

Tinsa smiled mischievously. "I just spent all day with a man." She cautiously said, wanting to keep them on their toes. She didn't want them jumping to conclusions either, so she added, "The man that Kyle sent to me." She smiled wickedly at Kyle. "I just came by to say thank you." She did a curtsy and turned to leave. "Oh, and by the way," She turned back

around and faced them. "We are setting up our friends with dates for your grand celebration!" Tinsa was glowing.

"Who?" Kyle asked. His brow was creasing at her games. "Well, we, I mean I, thought of Latell and Carieve when Ganter asked me to accompany him here. I assume that we are invited?" Tinsa asked. "Yes, of course."- Kyle and Robbie said in unison, without hesitation. "Then sweet Ganter, thought of Revie and Remid when I mentioned them."

"Swell." Kyle said.

"You do realize that with the rest of us attending, you will also need to find Nalame and Tenger, to invite them also, right?"

"Right." Kyle smiled at her.

"Yes, because a celebration isn't a celebration without them." Robbie added.

"Actually, everyone from both kingdoms is invited. Tell you what, why don't we put you in charge of informing the public?" Kyle asked Tinsa.

"Wow! Really! Awesome!" Tinsa exclaimed. She jumped up and down. "I would absolutely love to! Trust me, you won't be disappointed." She ran off before they could change their minds.

Kyle sighed. "Are all of your friends like this?" He asked her. Robbie laughed. "Only on good days." He kissed her lips and they went back inside.

It was a day's ride between the kingdoms. Ganter urged his horse to go faster. He wanted to be in the service of his master, but also in the company of Tinsa.

Ganter entered the Grand Hall and found Balcor dining with his wife alone. Sariah was much better, now that the spell on her had been broken. "Excuse me, sir, madame, I didn't mean to interrupt." He began to walk away backward.

"Nonsense."-Balcor motioned him forward. "Come back here, Ganter. Come and tell me, what news?"

Ganter curtsied again.-"Sire, you will be pleased to know that I have established it. There will be a grand celebration of her majesty, the Queen. It has been requested that myself, Revie, and Remid, should accompany you on this journey. Along with the lovely Duchess Sariah."

"Wonderful." He breathed as if a heavy burden had been lifted off of his chest. "Wonderful." Balcor took a great big bite from his chicken leg and spoke with his mouth full. "Go and prepare the horses and the staff." He swallowed his half-chewed food. "Tell

Revie and Remid of this change." He gulped down some wine. "We shall leave here on the marrow."

The great hall had to be thoroughly cleansed, before they even thought of decorating it. It hadn't been used in almost twenty years. The time and effort into it were well worth it. Even the servants who had stayed -had forgotten how truly magnificent it was.

Red draperies were then hung from ceiling beams. They swung delicately to the floor. The draperies were then tied with ribbon, back just enough to make a flowy effect. The granite walls could be seen behind them. The blue-stained, hard wood floors remarkably contrasted with the draperies.

People floated as if on air, to the music around them. The celebration was going to be incredible. Everyone was dancing and having a wonderful time, in preparation. The smell of the feast was intoxicating. Robbie's stomach growled.

Quail was the main course, followed by lobster and trout. Every dessert imaginable was being set on tables around the dining hall. The tables were anywhere from ten to fifty feet long. Each table in the dining area was surrounded by twelve to one hundred and seventy-five chairs. Almost six hundred people will be attending. Peasants, royals, and servants alike, were welcome.

Suddenly there was a great wind. It threw open the doors. A black figure appeared in the breezeway. Black soot made a face. "You fools! You haven't seen the last of me!" Movada's voice boomed across the walls. His laughter bounced around the room, even above the music. His presence mocked their peace.

"Kyle ran to the doorway. He closed it from the great wind with the help of three men. The back soot fell in a heaping pile on the floor. Movada's figure was gone, but his laughter remained.

A few minutes passed and people were silent or whispering quietly about what had just happened. The door opened and some of the people gasped. Villae burst in and stopped to look at everyone staring at her. "What's going on here? You all look like you've seen a ghost?" She found her sister's gaze in the back of the room. "I thought I was coming to a party!" She said sarcastically. She placed her hands on her hips.

Clairance laughed. Soon, Robbie and Kasde joined her. Kyle looked at them thoughtfully. He introduced himself, to whom he presumed to be the crazy aunt, from the forest. Villae shook his hand and then let go. She spun a large circle and thrust out her hands.

Magic flew from her fingertips in rainbow streaks. Blue, purple, and fluorescent pink swirled around the room. Music began from no place in particular. Transparent pastel streams of color burst through the air in a great mist. Fairies appeared all along it.

The whole kingdom of Whispershire united. All were one large Kingdom. One body, one mind, and one soul. The soul of a kingdom that could weather the storms as they pass. A kingdom that would last forever. The fairies, magic, and all.

Clairance and Villae helped move the heavy stuff with their magic. They prepared for the great party, in haste. Robbie was coming into the room from the kitchen. Kyle rushed to her. "Did you see or hear what happened?" He asked.

"Movada is a demon." Robbie replied. "We knew this. We just have to be cleverer when we kill him this time." She smiled at her husband. Her mother came to her side and hurriedly agreed. Robbie took in the sight of Villae and the fairies. "You're here! Out in the open!" She exclaimed.

Villae laughed. "It is my niece's party." She sneered at Kyle. "Or am I not welcome here?"

Kyle took Villae's hand. He gently kissed it. "All are welcome." He told her. She smiled at his gesture; and slowly curtsied. –He was also confused about all of the magic that had been aspiring recently. He nodded as he looked around, thinking. "And now there are even fairies in my castle." Robbie laughed. "You'll get used to it." She told him.

Kyle cast her a side glance. He smiled mischievously.-"And when will the rest of your friends be getting here?" He laughed. She wiggled her eyebrows at him. "Soon, Love, soon."

The villages were in an uproar of bliss. People were gathering their best produce, crafts, and baked goods, for gifts. It had been fifty years since Whispershire had a new Queen. They talked amongst themselves saying "how beautiful she is," and "she's so perfect for this."

The weather was cooperating nicely as well. There was a slight cool breeze, and just enough cloud shadows, to make it very nice outside. Flower petals flew through the air, as tree leaves rustled a tune. The women sang as they toiled. It had only been a few weeks since Movada's death, and already Whispershire was becoming its old self. Kyle had dealt justly with Movada's men. He had judged them according to their works that he saw.-Some pleaded with him to return to his service. Most of the men had souls that were tainted with evil. He could feel their lies coming through their skin. Those men were hanged.

Robbie was taking in everything around her. She beamed at the Royal Gardens. Fairies flew in and out now, helping things grow. This place was truly magical. Clairance and Kasde were also adjusting to palace life. They jumped in and helped where they could. Robbie and Kyle did also. They had lived a life of servitude. In their eyes everyone was equal. They just had more responsibilities.

Nelame had popped in a few times, to see her friends. Tenger was working the fields. She offered her relationship advice to Robbie. Robbie had rolled her eyes and smiled. She is a married woman now. They talked about how to ignite their passion; and keep their man happy. They would still laugh and blush at the subject.

Kyle was interviewing servants and staying busy with the courts. He had to make sure that the allies of his father were still true to their word. He was a wise King. Kyle had thought to bring Ganter in as his advisor, next. Ganter was loyal and had proved himself worthy of the title.

It also helped that he wanted to move closer to Tinsa. Balcor should have no objections. Kyle was also starting a school for the children; or any who wished to study. He thought of making Nelame a teacher. Robbie needed a friend close. His thoughts turned to Tivico. He missed him. Kyle smiled with sad eyes. He shook it off and returned to his paperwork.

The parchment was on old skins that had been dried. The ink was made of crushed berries. He wrote with the quill end of a hawk's feather. Warg had taught him how to read and write. He was grateful to the old man. Warg's health was steadily going downhill. He was rounding the corner of death, in his seventies.

Villae was very curious. She emerged everywhere, all at once. She went where she pleased; -when she wanted to do it. Kyle hadn't quite figured her out yet. She emerged and asked. "Have you made any provisions for me yet?" She cackled and disappeared.-Kyle shook his head at the interruption; but continued to work.

The servant girls of the castle had finished the decorations in the dining hall. It was breathtaking. A seamstress from the village had made Robbie gowns, that would be for the occasion and for everyday use. She had also sewn Kyle some matching tunics and vests.-Kyle had paid her in silver chunks.

The treasury was full of unrefined precious jewels, silver, and gold. Movada had only spent money on his drinking habits. He hadn't paid any of the workers; and collected taxes from the people. Kyle was figuring out a way to compensate for the unjust treatment of the people.

He invented a separate wage system, with the help of Robbie and her parents. Each person would be paid according to a finished task. Each task would be worth a different amount. Kyle refused to accept any work from anyone, that was free. He rebuffed adhering to a system of slavery. The people would trade and barter goods. Kyle would pay them for it.

He insisted on giving the land owners profits to better their crops. The field workers had told him a few good ideas, about water usage and canals. It would take a lot of work, but be beneficial in the end. Kyle had brought in masonry workers and blacksmiths. He wanted useful tools to aid the farmers. Wooden plows towed behind horses often broke.

Kyle sat back in his chair. He looked around his office, placing his arms on the chair's support rests. He took a deep breath. He was tired of politics for today.-He craned his neck, popping it on both sides. He stretched his shoulders and back, before he stood. He rolled the parchment into scrolls, and locked them in a wooden box.

Kyle wondered where his wife was. He desired her company. He thought of her sweet lips and how her body had responded to his. His heartbeat quickened. He swallowed the saliva that had formed. Kyle walked away from his study to find her.

Kyle found Robbie wandering the gardens. He watched her from the entrance. She moved with grace and eloquence. She smelled the flowers and played with the fairies. Kyle smiled. Robbie felt someone watching her. She turned to see who it was. She smiled at her husband. Robbie walked toward Kyle with haste. She wrapped her arms around his neck and kissed him. She sighed when she pulled away. "I love it here," she breathed into his ear.

Kyle chuckled. "Good, I would have it no other way."-He laughed again softly as he kissed her cheek. "What have you been up to today?" he asked her. Kyle grabbed her hand and led her to a nearby bench. He sat and pulled her into his lap.

The silk of Robbie's gown tickled his face as she came down on top of him. Kyle smiled mischievously. He wrapped his arms around her tightly. He squeezed her breasts into his face. Robbie laughed. "Stop. We are outside!" She panicked looking around.

"And? We are outside. We are married and we own the grounds." Kyle responded by doing it again. He nuzzled the flesh between her breasts, moving his head back and forth as he did so. Robbie playfully smacked his arm. "Kyle!" He chuckled into her flesh. She tried to move away and he held her still. Kyle pushed her down a way and held her head into his chest. Her feet were dangling off of the bench.

Robbie sighed and giggled. Her fingers found their way to his chest. His tunic left a perfect opening for her fingertips to graze his skin. He leaned his head back and moaned. "Robbie," He breathed into her hair. "Let's go upstairs."-Kyle stood and held his wife in his arms. He carried her to the end of the garden. Robbie clung to him. She breathed in his scent heavily. They were intoxicated with each other.

Kyle put her down at the garden entrance. Robbie turned and kissed him on the lips. She playfully scratched at his chest, where her fingers toyed with him. Robbie sent him a seductive glance when she looked into his eyes. He groaned.

Robbie turned and ran. "Catch me if you can!" She exclaimed. Her blue, silk, gown flowed behind her like a ribbon in the wind. She sprinted into the castle taking the stairs two at a time. Kyle knew the castle's secrets; he took another way. Robbie almost knocked over some of the servants, running down the corridor.

Kyle went through the kitchen. He used the stairwell to the servants' quarters that led to his office. The other side of the office went into the bedroom, where his bride would be coming soon. Robbie came through the doorway and closed the doors behind her. She caught her breath, leaning her forehead against the frame. She hadn't noticed that he had beaten her there.

Kyle came up behind her and grabbed her around the waist. She screamed. Kyle laughed. "It's just me," he told her.-He moved his hands up her body to cup her breasts, as he kissed down her back. His fingers moved quickly to the ties that held her dress together.

Robbie's heartbeat was fluttering wildly. She gasped as her dress hit the floor. Kyle started undoing the corset, hastily. His hungry eyes and mouth took in every inch of her as he did so.

Kyle turned her toward him. He studied her naked body ravenously. Robbie reveled in the looks that he gave her. She stood naked and proud before him. Her nipples perked at his gaze. She unconsciously shivered.

Kyle reached for her. He took her hand and led her to the enormous bed. Robbie sat, perched on the edge. She watched as he ripped the tunic up and over his head. His muscles flexed as he moved. She watched in

fascination as he undressed before her. She licked her lips as she examined his tan lines. His breeches fell to the floor in a heap. He moved to her. His mouth claimed hers.

Kyle kissed her passionately as he laid her back on the bed. His hands roved over her body freely. Robbie greedily felt his flesh under her hands. Their kiss deepened. Their breathing became labored and erratic. Robbie felt herself melting as a pool started between her thighs. Kyle captured one taut nipple in his mouth, he sucked and bit at it gently before moving on to the other one.

Kyle pushed her further onto the bed with his knee between her legs. Robbie moaned. Her center throbbed. She felt his erection grow against her leg. Kyle looked into her eyes as he centered himself above her. Robbie opened herself up to him. She gasped as his member entered her opening. Kyle groaned. He tried to enter her and let her get used to his girth. She gasped and bucked against him as she stretched, moving it more inside of her. Kyle responded by entering her all the way. He pulled back slowly, enjoying the feel of her warmth and tightness, around his engorged member.

Kyle moaned and captured her mouth with his as he drove into her again. They moved their hips in unison, in opposite directions. They crashed their bodies back together. She could feel him hitting her cervix. At first it was painful, but the more he did it, she felt euphoria. He touched places inside of her that she didn't know existed. Robbie gasped and moaned.

Kyle pushed himself faster and harder, opening her thighs more. He pushed her legs up over his shoulders as he drove further into her. She exploded cum all over his hard cock. She whimpered as her body shook with ecstasy. Kyle pushed into her, again and again, kissing her hard on the mouth, between panting and moaning. His cock grew with its need to blow. Robbie gasped, half sighed and half moaned all at the same time. He exploded into her core. His body shook. The sweat dripped from both of them coating the blanket on the bed.

Kyle let his member drain all of his fluids into her, before he pulled away and rolled off of her. He panted and breathed into her back as he pulled her close. Kyle kissed down her back as he caressed her body. Robbie lay next to him, sticky and wet.

The staff heard the commotion and had hot water and towels at the ready. Kyle pulled on his breeches and covered Robbie with a sheet; before he let them enter. The large tub in their room was soon full of hot water. The servants left them to bathe.

Kyle reached for Robbie. She slowly walked toward the tub. She was sore and leaking. "I love you," he said. "I hope I didn't hurt you."-His eyes were full of concern. He didn't want her to be afraid to make love to him. "Please, let me take care of you."

Robbie nodded her head and stepped into the tub. Lowering herself into the water, she sighed. "I love you too," she breathed. Robbie was slowly getting used to this. Kyle was a generous lover. He always wanted to care for her afterwards. She felt her euphoria edify her feelings of love for him. She had known love before, but not like this.

Kyle rubbed her muscles as he applied the bathing oils. He let his fingers dance across her smooth flesh. Robbie moaned again. His touch was inebriating.-Kyle washed her off with buckets of water that had been generously supplied. He kissed her skin as he did so. He

71

played with her opening as he washed the cum away. He inserted one finger, and with her response to him, he inserted another. He fingered her pussy in the water, washing it out, for them to do it again later.

Robbie was enthralled with his movements. She wondered where he had learned everything that he knew how to do with her. She let the thought pass as she enjoyed his touch and his movements. He massaged her lower lips with his fingers and playfully pinched at her butt cheeks. Robbie smiled up at him. He leaned down and kissed her gently.

Robbie rose from the tub and donned a towel. She led Kyle into the tub so she could do the same for him. She massaged his skin with the bathing oils. She played with his muscles in his arms and shoulders. Her hands moved down his back slowly. She caressed his chest and torso. Robbie felt every inch of him. She toyed with his butt as she rubbed and pinched gently, as he had done to her. Robbie felt the muscles in his legs flex as she rubbed in the oils. Kyle kicked away her hands as she tickled his feet. Robbie giggled.

She reached for the buckets of water to rinse him. She leaned over the tub to grab them. Kyle caught her breast in his mouth as she did so. Robbie gasped and almost dropped it from surprise. She dumped the whole thing over his head. Kyle gasped. "What the hell?"

Robbie laughed. "You caught me off guard," She replied. "Besides, you deserved it for that!" She laughed again

"You tickled my feet!" He exclaimed. Kyle laughed out loud. "Minx," he teased.

Robbie laughed again. She rinsed him off and helped him out of the tub. She watched with fascination as he stood, naked and wet, in front of her. She licked her lips and grabbed another towel. She began to rub him down with it, drying him off. She kissed everywhere the towel left. Kyle moaned. "Be careful, dear wife. I may take you again."-He chuckled. His eyes told her that he spoke the truth. Robbie was enthralled with his supernatural member, but she didn't want another escapade this soon. She dried him more roughly. Finished, she appraised her work. Robbie smiled at him.

Kyle caught her around the waist and pulled her to him. He dropped her towel on the floor. He loved the feel of her nakedness against him. He hugged her tightly for a few moments before releasing her. He kissed her mouth and let her go to her clothing.

They hurriedly got dressed. There were more pressing matters to attend to, where they couldn't be alone, or naked. Kyle contemplated abolishing the law that opposed lewdness. He chuckled at the thought.

Robbie smiled at him as she tied the laces to her sandals. Kyle watched her every movement. He was thoroughly infatuated. He licked his lips and swallowed.

The day was quickly running its course. There was to be a big celebration. Kyle's stomach growled as the scent from the kitchen wafted up to their room. A trumpet blew outside announcing that a visitor had arrived.

Kyle raised his eyebrows. He smiled at Robbie and replaced his tunic and boots. "Just in time." He chuckled softly.- Robbie brushed the knots from her hair; and used magic to pull it into a fashionable updo.- She wore a gown of green gossamer lace that covered a white silk bodice. She placed her crown on her head; and finished her appearance with earrings and a necklace of emeralds.

Kyle sucked in his breath through his teeth. "God, you are beautiful." He sighed and walked out the door to greet their guests.

CHAPTER NINE

Balcor waved up from his carriage. Revie, Remid, and Ganter were on horseback next to it.- Remid's horse bucked and reared upward as Kyle approached. Remid quickly got it under control. The brown and gray mare was exquisite. She was in shape. Her muscles were defined and pulsing from the run. The horse snorted.

Kyle walked up to her and petted her nose. She blew out of her nostrils in response. Her eyes were wild. Kyle looked at the men. "Get these horses some water." He commanded. "You may place them all in the stalls. There are water troughs and hay in there." He nodded to his friends.

They nodded back and began to take their horses to the stalls, including the ones that were pulling the carriage. Balcor and Sariah emerged from the carriage, just before they were pulled away with it. Sariah was glad to be out in the open air. "That was quite the ride." She stated, as she stretched. She was wearing a gown of cherry red, accompanied by rubies. Her brown hair was pulled atop her head, with ringlets surrounding her face.

Balcor's carriage was also finely decorated with his riches. He wore a cape matching his wife. Balcor carried a walking stick that was large. It has an engraved eagle on the top. It had been blazed with fire in places and then finished with a rich, oaken polish. He walked in step with Sariah toward the castle.

Clairance and Kasde rushed out to meet them. They were still very much in the manner of servitude. Ganter retrieved the luggage from the carriage; and brought it to the suite that they would be staying in. Phoebe still hung onto Clairance's shoulder. Sariah was taken aback by the magical creatures buzzing about. She had heard rumors of them, but never actually seen a fairy.

Kasde led them to the dining hall, where a luncheon had been prepared. Once seated, a few new girls from the village brought out place settings for them. Kyle had hired a new bunch of servants to see to the guests' needs. He wanted everyone to feel welcomed; and cared for. The celebrations would ensure that the people loved their new queen. Kyle firmly believed that love would aspire more determined workers; and a better morale for the kingdom.

Robbie, of course, stood with him on it. They wanted a kingdom like that of Rosecco and Zipurda. They also wanted to do better for the people. Robbie came to sit at the table. Sariah was mesmerized by the dining hall's transformation. "You all have done so much!" She exclaimed.

Robbie smiled at her. "It was a lot to be reckoned with." She smiled wider as a fairy came to sit on her chair. "Of course, we had a lot of help."

The fairy winked and nodded, and flew away. Sariah raised her eyebrows as she smirked. "There is magic here." Robbie told her, laughing at her expression.

Roast pheasant was placed before them with boiled potatoes and carrots. The aroma was heavenly. Robbie hadn't realized how hungry she was. The servant girl poured water into her goblet as she smiled, humming a familiar tune. Robbie nodded and thanked her, followed by Kasde and Clairance.

Kyle and his family did the same.-They were eating alone for the moment. No one else was allowed into the dining hall until the feast. Everything had its own intricate place holding. The men riding with Balcor ate in the kitchen. They chatted and flirted with the staff before moving back outside. Revie and Remid were curious as to their dates, but they couldn't get any information out of Ganter.

Ganter laughed at their requests for information. He finished his tasks at the castle and almost ran to the village to see Tinsa. He was infatuated by her beauty and boldness. He found her securing a wagon for delivery. Some of the goods rolled off of the top as she tried to tie it together. Ganter moved in closer, catching them before they hit the ground.

"Well done. Amazing reflexes!" Tinsa laughed, seeing him catch them. She finished her half hitch, and walked past him to the other side. Her bosom brushed against his back as she moved, sending waves of electricity through them both. She smiled but kept to her task. Ganter placed the parcels into her wagon, where he could see to stuff them without damage. He admired her handiwork.

"Well done yourself."-He whistled. "You tie knots better than a boy scout." He complimented her, smirking.

She looked him over and rolled her eyes. "You could've helped me; if you had been here faster." She teased by pushing her lips into a pout. Ganter licked his lips and swallowed. Tinsa laughed at the response. "Not that I had needed any help." She added.

The man at the next booth laughed at their exchange. A horse rode past kicking up dust. Tinsa brushed it off and grabbed her wagon cart by the handles. "Are you coming?"-She asked Ganter.

He smiled at her and obligingly grabbed the handle on the other end. "You bet I am. I would pull it myself if it meant more time with you." He answered.

She blushed as she smiled back. She gave him a side-eye glance and giggled.- This was their sixth outing together. She was enjoying

his company. They stepped together making the wheels pull from their hold in the dirt. "We are taking this one to Nelame." She told him. Ganter beamed. "Good. I was wondering when I was going to meet these friends of yours. You know that my comrades are demanding information about them." He chuckled. "It was easy to remain mysterious, as I didn't have any of the answers that they wanted." He looked at her. Tinsa laughed. "Oh, just pull the wagon." She said flatly. She saw his perplexing stare. "You all will be acquainted soon enough."-A breeze blew in from the west. Tinsa's hair flew around her face. She blew at it from her mouth; and shook her head around.

Ganter laughed. "Do we need to stop?" He asked her.

She shook the hair free from her vision. It coated her head sideways; as if she had brushed it like that. "Hell no!" She bellowed. "We keep moving. It is harder to restart once you stop. Especially if you have a slope to cover." She scolded.

There was a small hill to overcome on the way to Nalame's cottage. Tinsa and Ganter stepped together. It was an easier task with two. Tinsa was enjoying having company and help. She wouldn't tell him that, though. She had grown accustomed to being an independent woman. Ganter would have to work hard, to show her that she needed a man. He would also have to convince her father.

Nelame was home, weeding her flowerbed. She brushed the hair from her face, as she pushed away the bead of sweat forming at her forehead. Her gloved hand left a dirt streak across her face. She looked up from her chore and greeted them. Nelame sniffled a bit when she stood. The dust and pollen had settled on her fair skin. Her red curls fluttered momentarily in the breeze. Her freckles glistened in the sun.

"Hello there!" Nelame smiled at them as they came to a stop next to her.

"Nelame. I have your delivery." Tinsa beamed at her friend. "And who's this, that you have strapped in like a mule?" Nelame asked, teasing her.

Ganter rolled his eyes at their banter. He loosened his grip from the hand cart wagon and eased it down. Ganter moved slowly under the rail and stretched when he straightened. "I am Ganter." He reached out his hand to shake hers.

Nelame stretched her gloved hand into his. Ganter bowed slightly and kissed the top of her hand. She blinked her eyes at Tinsa, then wiggled her eyebrows. "I am Nelame.'" She curtsied slightly from his mannerisms.

Ganter noticed the exchange of expressions from the girls. "I am a servant to the Duke of Vole Tirfs, King Kyle has asked me to be his assistance at the castle." He felt the need to explain himself.

Tinsa and Nelame looked at each other and laughed out loud. Ganter was not sure if he had said something humorous. "You do not have to be all formal, we are not royals."- Tinsa laughed. She began uncovering her cart. She smiled at nothing in particular. She tried to keep her face hidden beneath the wagon covering as she stared at Ganter, amused.

Nelame moved next to Tinsa and grabbed a gunny sack of corn flour. She tossed Tinsa a knowing smile as she threw it over her shoulder. Tinsa smiled back, trying not to blush, as they communicated silently with their eyes. Ganter ignored them and hurdled a heaping pile of dried corn husks into his arms.

"Where would you like it?" Ganter asked her walking toward the cottage.

Nelame walked past him and opened a tiny gate. Chickens ran past her feet as she entered a small barn in the backyard. There was a high shelf above the hay loft. "Up there." She conveyed it to him. She began to climb a wooden ladder.

Ganter stopped her. "I will do it." Nelame moved to the side. She was supposed to always allow chivalry. She didn't mind.

"Thank you, Ganter." Nelame said, handing him the flour, once he had lain down his load. She looked to Tinsa who was coming in with more. "Quite the gentleman you have found," Nelame told her.

Tinsa moved next to the ladder. She handed the barrel of seeds to Ganter. She watched his muscles flex as he pushed them upward. Her eyes glistened with lust and joy.

Nelame noticed. "About time." She announced, nodding at her friend. Her apron swished as she moved away. Her light - colored dress was covered in dirt and grass stains. To the right side of her little barn, she gathered some eggs from the hens nesting, perch coops. She placed the eggs gently in her apron pockets.

Tinsa followed her into the cottage. Ganter meandered the property and waited for either an invitation, - or for the return of the girls. He was impressed with the white-painted cobble rock. The house was quaint and impressive in its structure. The mortar was painted over with blue hues. The house kind of looked like a flower.

Tinsa and Nelame returned to the outdoors laughing. Ganter smiled at them. This was the second friend of hers that he had gotten the pleasure

of meeting. It was the other two that he was still curious about. The banquet should be fantastic, he thought to himself.

"Ready?" Tinsa asked him. "I have other deliveries to make today." She moved to her place in front of the empty wagon cart. She waved "goodbye" to Nelame as Ganter took his place next to her.

"Nice to meet you," Ganter bobbed his head at Nelame. She smiled in return. He gripped the cart and followed Tinsa's lead. They headed back to the village to reload.

"Your friends are nice." Ganter told her. "Am I going to meet these mysterious women before the party?"

Tinsa laughed. "We'll see." She teased while she smirked at him, raising her eyebrows.

Back at the castle Revie and Remid were wondering the same thing. They were talking together in the stables, wondering about what Ganter had gotten them into. He had not even described the girls to them, only saying that they had dates, and it was requested by the new queen.

Remid reached into a watering trough, getting his hands wet. He pushed his hair back. It was short on the back and sides, and hung down into his eyes from the top. His eyes were a light brown with gold and green flecks in them. His skin was tanned from working in the sun.-His muscles flexed as he raked his hands through his hair.

"Are you worrying about tonight?" Revie asked him, watching Remid as he fidgeted around the stables.

Remid shook the water off and refixed his hair. "Aren't you?" Revie smirked and chewed a piece of straw. He flicked it with his straight, white teeth. "I've no problem with the ladies." He confidently stated. His dark brown hair was shoulder-length and wavy. His eyes were a golden brown, accompanied by a deep sultry voice. "That's not it." Remid replied. "I have not been invited to a formal banquet, as a guest." He sighed and played with his hair some more. "I do not know how to dance."

Revie laughed out loud. He smacked his thigh and stamped his foot at the same time. "How? Ha. It's not hard!" He moved to the other side of Remid. "Grab that mare." He pointed to a small dapple-gray horse. "I'll show you."

Remid got a hold of the horse and put a bit in her mouth. Revie grabbed some reins and a lead rope. Remid went to climb on top. Revie stopped him. "No. Here to the side." He pointed next to her on the ground.

Remid stood next to the mare. Revie moved the lead rope so that her feet went back and forth instead of forward. "Don't let her step on your feet. And keep up." He moved her faster and then had her twirl around. Remid dodged the movement and came back to her side.

"Move here, in front and try it again with your hands on her neck." Revie told him. Remid did as instructed. The horse moved with the rope but was confused about the two men. She snorted at him, but they were dancing. Revie laughed. "See. It's easy."

Remid moved back laughing. He walked to the trough and washed his hands and face. He dried them with his tunic, also trying to remove the horse snot that had been blown on him.

The men put the horse and tack back in the barn. Remid brushed the mare down and gave her some water. "Thank you." He told her. He laughed again as she nuzzled his tunic. He petted the top of her head and scratched behind her ears. She neighed her appreciation.

People were arriving at the castle now in groups. They were dressed in their finest arrays. Servants were practically running to gather baskets and horses. Gifts of all shapes and sizes were being taken into the throne room. The kitchen staff was working overtime creating confections and treats to cover the tables that lined the walls of the great dining hall.

Robbie was ready. She was peering over the crowds from a balcony that looked out from her study parlor. She saw her mother and father, and her friends from her village. Nelame and Tenger had just waltzed through the doors. They were dressed alike in blue. Tenger looked like a gentleman, he held her elbow while they walked and greeted people. Robbie smiled at the thought.-She nodded down to Nelame who had just seen her.

Nelame looked up with her head and smiled. Tenger did the same, noticing her motion. He had his hair slicked back and tied into a ponytail. His face was partially shaven, all except for his chin. -He looked the part of a lord's man.-Nelame had jewels on her hands and wrists. A small chain necklace was around her neck accentuating the curves of her shoulders. The bodice of her dress was low. It had lace around the edges of her bosom. Her sleeves were puffed out and hung from her biceps. Nelame's figure was slender, - and perfectly defined by her chosen wardrobe.

Keesha flew to her and kissed her on the cheek. Nelame winked at her new little friend; and giggled as she flew away. Nelame had only seen the fairies once, before, and here they were everywhere. Villae's magic was encircled everywhere. Scented, colored mists came into the air from fountains, and fell back into them.

People were astonished at all that had been done. The room itself was magnificent. The magic added to its prowess. Just past the dining hall was a large ballroom. It had also been enchanted. Fairies hung ribbons and flitted back and forth on them, like slides for children. They flew in and out of the fountains of color, splashing the fragrance through the air as they flew.

A band of violins and cellos started playing music. Balls of light danced around them. Torches lit along the walls as if on cue. Villagers started dancing to the music. It was turning out to be a graceful, elegant occasion, completed with unimaginable beauty.

Kyle went upstairs to collect his wife. He donned his crown and had Robbie do the same. They came together down the winding wooden staircase. King and Queen. They paused at the bottom stair. "Thank you all for coming." Kyle started to speak. "We could not have asked for better friends and family for support on this occasion." He looked at each of them in the room. "Your Queen, Robbie, of Whispershire." He announced her, and held their hands in the air.

The people cheered and applauded. Robbie smiled and nodded to them all. When they stopped Robbie nodded again to the music makers. They struck up their chords. People posed to dance. Someone's clapping was getting louder. It continued through the music and grew louder still. Robbie and Kyle looked through the crowd. It was not coming from any of the guests.

Clapping became thunderous. The music stopped. The people hushed each other and started to go outside. They were covering their ears to get away from the noise. Evil laughter surrounded them.

"Where is he?" Kyle shouted, frantically looking around. His face was serious. The guards came in waving their swords around. They formed a protective circle around the king and queen.

Villae pushed herself through the crowds leaving the ballroom. She spun her magic to silence the noise. The side effects were that now no one could hear anything. It was as if life had become slow motion. There was no sound and almost no movement. Movada's form showed itself in the middle of the ballroom floor. Robbie gasped inaudibly. Kasde moved toward the table at the far wall. Clairance was at his heels.

Villae raised her hands and pulled energy from the room. The fairies froze. The lights dimmed. She shot electricity from her fingertips toward Movada's shadow. Clairance and Kasde joined her.

Robbie felt the pull of their magic and raised her arms. The guards ducked.

Robbie closed her eyes. "Kyle, sit down!" She yelled at him. "Please I don't want you hurt," She begged him to just listen. He sat on the staircase surrounded by his men. They had their weapons drawn from all angles around him. Robbie pulled the energy from the jewels in the room. She shot her magic toward him as well.

Movada's laughter broke through the sphere of silence. He spun his black form with ash and soot from the torches. A demon scowl could be seen forming in the center of his form. Red glowing eyes came next, followed by claws, horns, and tail. The demon emerged. Black soot fell to the ground. Power surged from them.

Movada's laughter became more and more volatile. He screeched and writhed. His claws ran through the hardwood floor. The air smelled of burning sulfur. The demon grew bigger and broke free from their magic. Villae growled and grabbed her sister's hand.

Movada stretched his power toward Robbie. He wrapped his hands around her throat. She brought her arms down trying to get him off of her. Kyle rushed toward her only to be flung back against the wall. The guards threw daggers and shot arrows. Movada was strong. He shielded himself against the weapons.

Fairies attacked him using their teeth. Movada's demon growled as its eyes glowed. Villae was not powerful enough against him. She needed her spells and cauldron. Clairance found a way through the shield. She stabbed the beast in the stomach. Blood splashed her. Movada was able to see who she was and who she had been. He recognized her as the woman from the Vole Tirfs, the night that he was poisoned.

Movada threw all of his magic toward Clairance. He forced her to the ground. A snake-like tongue emerged from this demon's head. He licked her face up the side as he pinned her to the floor. Robbie regained her breath. Kyle ran to her. Robbie engaged the jewels in the room to enhance her power. She combined her magic with Villae's. Robbie shot a large ball of electric energy into Movada.

His skin sizzled. The demon let out a hiss. His body shook as he tried to remain in control. Clairance stabbed him again from beneath. Movada looked her in the eyes promising to return. The demon evaporated. Clairance sat up and wiped her face.

Villae and the fairies cleaned up the blood, soot, and dust. Kasde helped Clairance to get some water. Kyle moved Robbie to do the same. They were going to need help. Kyle didn't know of any other kingdom that used magic, other than Soothsayers. Kyle's man ran to get the priest.

Tenger emerged through the doors with Nelame behind him. "What in the hell happened in here?" he asked.

"What in the hell is right" Robbie answered. "Movada was back as a demon!" She exclaimed. She glanced around the room. "He will be back, and we need to be ready. We need to be rid of him once and for all."-Kyle stated.

Tenger nodded his head looking around the room. The fairies were working overtime to make the room ready again for the people. The party would continue. They were not going to let Movada ruin anything for them, ever again. Tinsa and Ganter entered the room. They nodded their hellos and found Robbie and Kyle. Tinsa's gray eyes grew wide as noticed the marks around Robbie's throat.-"What the hell!" She exclaimed looking to throttle Kyle.

Robbie saw her stare go from her neck to Kyle. "Tinsa, No. It's not like that. We were attacked by Movada as a demon." She told her. Tinsa looked back at Robbie; as if she didn't believe what she was hearing. "A lot has happened." Robbie told her as she shook her head.

Ganter looked over the room. He saw the tear on Kyle's tunic. The look of horror on Clairance and Kasde's faces told him enough. He nodded to the guards and the men in the room. He didn't say a word. Ganter kissed Tinsa on the cheek and left the room.

He ran to the cellar. He looked over the wine. He found the bottle of poison that he had purchased. He saw the markings of an old crone. He took the bottle to the throne room. He was going to put it down and then go ask for a meeting, but he thought better of it. He placed it under his tunic in a makeshift pocket.

Ganter came back into the ballroom. He nodded to Kyle who came to him straightaway. "We also need Balcor and the guards." Ganter told him. "We need a meeting to discuss the aspects of killing Movada's soul." Ganter was upset with himself for not considering what he had done in more detail.

The men moved to the throne room. Tenger joined them. Revie, Remid, Ganter, Balcor, and Kyle sat at the table. The guards moved to surround them. Ganter showed them the bottle of poison. He had them note the marks of the crone. He needed them to find her. "She has to tell us how to fix this!" Ganter exclaimed. "It was supposed to kill him. All of him!" Ganter moved to the side of the room. "I saw her at the edge of the forest glade. We had a meeting on one of my trips back and forth."

"I will go and find her." Tenger offered. "I am not really the celebrate and dance sort of guy anyway." He laughed nervously.

"Nelame would have your head." Kyle teased him. "I will let nothing get in the way of celebrating my queen! He wanted to interrupt this for us. I will not allow it. We will find the crone tomorrow. I do not believe he will be back today." Kyle told them.

Balcor agreed. "Ganter keep that bottle close. Don't let anyone get to it." He commanded him. The men hastily approved. Kyle dismissed them. He exchanged a look of concern with his uncle. Balcor shook his head and shrugged his broad shoulders. "Let's get back to the women, -before they start gossiping." Balcor told him. They all laughed as they exited the throne room into the hallway. They walked together toward the ballroom as if they didn't have a care in the world.

Tinsa had taken Robbie outside. Nelame followed. They were waiting not so patiently for Latell and Carieve to arrive. "So, are you going to be honest about what is going on here?" Tinsa asked Robbie, tapping her foot.

Robbie glared at her friend for a moment. She rolled her eyes. "I have been experiencing things that I didn't know were possible." She answered. She blushed when she saw Tinsa's toothy grin. "Not like that! Well, that too, but not what I was talking about!" Robbie shook her head. She inhaled a deep breath. "I would have to start at the beginning. I may as well wait for the others." She threw her hands into the air.

Carriages could be heard coming down the winding dirt road. Tinsa spotted a lantern inside of one. "I believe that they are here!" She told Robbie. They laughed as some other visitors walked past them to the garden latrine.

Robbie moved forward to see her friends. She wanted to talk about everything. At the same time, she didn't. She wanted her friends to know of the danger; but also wanted to keep them safely out of it. The entire kingdom now knew about magic, but they didn't know that it came from her family. She could trust them, right? Robbie sighed at her inner thoughts.

The carriage finally came to a stop, just next to the gravel pathway that led to the castle doors. Latell almost jumped from the carriage. She was ecstatic to be on the ground and not moving so fast. She wore a gown of dandelion yellow. It had large brown and green sunflowers on it. She wore a small jacket covered in white denim. It made her skin look slightly darker, and her freckles not as noticeable. She also wore quaint spectacles, with pink rims, that made her face a slightly different shape. They were pleasant looking, on her. She was nervous about meeting Ganter's friends.

Carieve stepped onto the carriage's rails. Her black boots could be seen just under the hem of her long, pink dress. It had little sequined roses going up one side to her waist in an S-shaped curve.

The waist was tapered in and came to just above her cleavage. She had a shawl covering her shoulders that was just a shade lighter. Her blonde hair had been curled and hung loosely. She smiled when her blue eyes met Robbie's.

The girls ran to embrace their friends. They had not seen each other since before Robbie went to Camo Forest. The four of them walked to the gardens. The pathways were lit by lanterns. Glowing balls of energy were feeding the plants, placed carefully by the fairies. Latell had to investigate it.-She sank almost to her knees. She squatted carefully, next to the plants and the glowing orbs. She went to place her finger into the orb. She was so intent on finding out what it was, and what it was doing; that she didn't hear Tinsa sneak up behind her and push her over into it.

Latell screamed. The girls laughed. Robbie helped her up and cleaned her off with a wave of her hand. The girls watched her fascinated. "Ok. Robbie I am tired of waiting. What is going on around here? How did you get magical powers all of a sudden? And the fairies?" Tinsa demanded to know.

Robbie smiled at them. She led her friends to the benches under the trees. They could look up to the moonlight. Robbie slowly explained everything to them, about the forest. Then she told them of how the fairies led her to her family. They had yet to see Villae.

"I thought your father was dead!" Carieve exclaimed. "Holy buckets! What a set-up! And with a Prince!" They squealed their excitement. "How lucky did you get?"

Robbie laughed. She still had to explain Movada's death and the mysterious appearances. When she had concluded, her stomach growled. "How do you kill a demon, not from this world?"-Latell asked, growing concerned for the safety of them all.

They looked at each other. No one knew.

Ganter came around the corner. He had been searching for his date; and her friends. "Ah, there you are." You said when he had come upon them.

Tinsa smiled at him. She introduced them to him. He smiled and bowed, the same as a formal gentleman. He winked at the girls. "You are both beautiful," he told them. "I would choose your dates wisely," he told them. "They are awaiting you in the dining hall." He offered his elbow to Tinsa. "My lady."-He expectantly waited for her. "We shall follow the rest of you inside."-He informed them.

Robbie laughed and bobbed her head. "Of course, sir."-She lifted her skirts and helped Latell and Carieve to stand.-She led them too the dining hall that was just past the gardens through the kitchen. She popped a tart into her mouth as they passed through.

In the dining hall the men were waiting by the table. They were laughing about something, and eating confections. They stopped messing around and stood still as the women approached. Revie caught sight of Carieve and his heartbeat quickened.

Latell studied Remid. Their eyes locked. She smiled shyly at him. Ganter came forward and made the introductions. The men bowed and kissed each hand. Robbie left her friends to mingle amongst each other. The musicians had reassembled under the balcony. They began to play as she entered the ballroom.

Kyle looked up from the discussion he was having with his uncle. He nodded to his wife as she approached. Kyle stood and took her by the hand. They began to dance gracefully across the floor. Minuet and Waltz's tunes came to life through the violins. Others soon joined them. The dance floor became alive with colors floating in sync. Ladies' gowns were twirling like butterflies on flowers. It was as if the room itself was spinning.

Revie danced with Carieve. Remid was dancing with Latell. Tinsa danced with Ganter. Kyle and Robbie were followed by Sariah and Balcor. Kasde took Clairance to the dancefloor as well. Servants danced together, as well as the villagers.

Fairies spun magic around. Everyone was having fun. The music changed drastically to a polka. Conga lines formed from the back. The ladies were dipped and twirled until they were dizzy. Men moved with grace and danced as equals to their partners. There was no class distinction. The servants danced as they were, in between filling goblets of wine; and bringing more food to the tables. The party was an extravagant success.

People were filtering into the dining hall as the meal was placed on the long tables. Robbie and Kyle made their way to their seats. Friends and family alike were seated around them. Quail and roast pigs were placed on serving trays, with vegetables and bread.

Kyle made the announcement that it was time to eat. He clinked a knife on his glass goblet and toasted to his wife. "We will make this kingdom great again! My beautiful wife, Robbie, and I, welcome you all to our home. Let the feasting begin!"

Laughter and cheers could be heard all around. Drunken speeches and toasts continued through the evening. Cakes and confections of all sorts emerged as if from nowhere. The working men tore into the prepared beats as if they were starving. Gentle ladies and men of stature picked at their plates delicately. When the party was over the villagers filtered

outside, waiting for their rides home. Balcor and Sariah drifted through the halls to their room.

Carieve and Latell stayed with their dates as they prepared horses to come and go. They were enthralled by the tasks at hand and seeing these men in their day-to-day element.-Ganter had ensured that they also had rooms to stay in. Robbie and Kyle retired for the night to their bedchamber, as did Clairance and Kasde.

A few good servants took over for Revie and Remid so that they may continue the evening with the women. Tinsa helped Ganter with luggage as well. She, too, was to stay the night. They ate and drank merrily. The party stopped its movement around one o'clock in the morning. Silence filled the castle.

CHAPTER TEN

Moonlight infiltrated through the glass windows. The fairies had all gone to sleep in the hay lofts. There was an eerie darkness that crept through the castle. It went room by room, searching for something, or someone.- Black shadow figures danced along the walls. Red and green eyes darted from the corners of the rooms.

The people in the castle were fast asleep, partly from the strong drink and partly from exhaustion. The shadow made its way up the stairs, leaving behind a trail of ash. Its eyes changed colors again when it found its specific target. The shadow formed a large black feline. It crept slowly forward. Its movements were even catlike. He purred as he leaped onto the bed. He stretched. His talons clawed into her and then stretched further to make fingers. His fingers wrapped around her throat as he moved on top of her.

He covered her mouth with a pillow case in his hand. She opened her eyes but she couldn't move or scream. Clairance willed herself to move. She twitched under him. Movada's form was almost completely solid. He cast a spell, binding Kasde into a deep sleep. He wouldn't be aware of anything.

"I told you. I demand that you are in my bed." Movada whispered in her ear. A snake-like tongue emerged from his mouth and trailed down her face. The hair was raised on her arms and neck. Movada lifted her nightshirt and spread her legs apart, using his thighs. -Clairance tried to fight him, but he was too strong. She was powerless in her state. Tears fell from her eyes as he forced his huge cock into her. He kissed down her face and neck. His saliva burned like venom on her skin.-He did not leave her or let her move until he had finished. She sobbed and cried, long after he had left. Kasde awoke to her weepy and shaking form. He saw the trail of soot that went into the bedroom from the hall. "What happened?" He asked her.

She demanded "a bath be brought in at once." She evaded his questions. She was in shock and felt shame, fear, and guilt. Kasde held her and tried his best to comfort her. She would not be consoled. She shook and cried more. "Get away from me!" She yelled. "Can't you see that I am filthy! I am defiled!" She howled and tore the nightshirt from her body. She threw it to him. "We are all powerless against him!"

The maids brought in the giant silver tub and steaming hot water. They rushed in and out. They didn't want to interrupt what they thought was a lover's quarrel. Clairance sobbed as she scrubbed her body. It wasn't enough. "I need a wire brush!" She screamed.

"No!" Kasde answered. "No, you do not. You will not tear off your skin! It will not make you feel better." He moved next to her. He rubbed lavender oil and eucalyptus on her body. He saw the scratches and finger marks. -Kasde swore under his breath. "Baby, we're going to figure this out," he said as he shook his head.

Kasde was outraged. He was trying to not show his emotions to his wife. She needed him to be strong. She was raped by a demon monster! She shook and cried. She held herself, intimately. She tried to scrub off the feeling of him. His feel, and his scent wouldn't leave her.

"Leave me." She told him. "I need to be alone."- She cried. Kasde stood and left the room. He stomped to Kyle and Robbie's room. He knocked lightly at first. He was shaking, trying to control the rage that he felt. He knocked louder. He pounded on the door with his fists when he didn't get an answer.

"Excuse me My Lord. They are in the foyer."-A servant came to him and explained that they were not in their room.

Kasde looked at the servant with tears in his eyes. "Thank you." He stammered. He sighed and fought the tears back. Kasde walked to the foyer. Kyle looked up. He was going to say "good morning," but changed his mind at Kasde's expression.

"What has happened?" Kyle asked, coming to him. He placed both hands on Kasde's shoulders. He tried to look him in the eye. Kasde didn't look up.

"Where is my mother?" Robbie asked, standing. The room went silent. Robbie panicked. She began to run to Clairance. Kasde stopped her. "Robbie, please. You should sit." He said, sniffling.

Kyle and Robbie stared at him with concern. They looked at each other. "Is she ok?" Robbie asked. Kasde didn't answer immediately. "Where is my mother? Is she dead?" Robbie demanded an answer.

Kasde swallowed. "Something bad has happened." The tears fell freely down his cheeks. "She is alive but might not wish to be." He shook his head.

Kyle shook him. "What the hell happened!?" Kyle demanded. Kasde looked up. He looked at Robbie and then back to Kyle. "Movada." That was all he said.

Robbie rushed from the room. No one could stop her this time. She ran straight to her mother's room. She did not knock. She ran in and locked the door behind her. "Mother!" She screamed. She ran around the room until she found her mother crying in a tub that was getting too cold to sit in. Robbie grabbed a towel. "Mother come on." Robbie held the towel out to her. "Please get out of that cold water and come here."

Clairance looked up. She had just now seen Robbie. She snapped to the present. She looked around her and shivered. Clairance stood and stepped out of the tub. Robbie wrapped her mother in the towel. She grabbed another to dry her hair. They moved toward the bed to sit. Clairance stared at it and wouldn't go any further.

Robbie saw the soot on the sheets. She could smell sulfur in the air. Robbie moved her mother away from it and sat her on the vanity chair. Clairance stared at the bed from the mirror glass.

Robbie ran to the bed and stripped it down to nothing. She wadded up the blankets and sheets and threw them on the floor. She went back to her mother. "Talk to me." Robbie said. She looked into her mother's tear-stained face. "Please, tell me what happened."

Clairance rubbed her arms to warm them. She remembered how the hair had stood on her arms and neck. She stared at her hands. She had never felt so powerless, so abandoned by herself. She looked at her daughter. "Robbie. We have to find a way to kill him!" She sniffled and more tears fell.-Clairance sobbed "I couldn't stop him! I couldn't move!" She cried and shook some more. Robbie held her.

"Movada was here! He raped me!" She yelled. "I couldn't scream. I couldn't fight back, and Kasde was next to me!" She screamed and cried and wrapped her arms around herself.-"Robbie, he must die!"

Robbie was enraged. Tears rolled down her face. She agreed with her mother. "Yes, he must."- Her mind went in a thousand different directions. How were they going to kill a demon spirit that could become tangible? How was her mother powerless against this monster? Why couldn't Kasde wake up and take him out? How did he keep getting in the castle?

Kyle was going over the same questions with Kasde, downstairs. Balcor came forward with the Bible. "This may be the only way." He placed it on the table in the office. Sariah ran to get the Priest.- Revie and Remid followed behind him, coming on from outside.

"What is going on here?" The priest asked. "I have preparations to make for service." He glanced at the men. They were somber. Kyle bowed his head. "Father, please." He looked him in the eye. "We have a supernatural conundrum."-He titled his head. "None of you here have experience with dark arts."

The priest was dumbfounded. "Make sense, boy, speak plainly." Kyle took a deep troubled breath. "Movada had returned in the form of a demon." He said as soberly as he could muster. He watched the priest's face turn distorted.

"Non-sense." The priest did not take kindly to this. He thought it was some sort of joke.-He shook his head and scolded them for messing with things that they could not know about.

Clairance emerged into the room. She bared her arms and legs for inspection by the priest. She showed him the bruises and cuts. Her skin was marked like burns everywhere that he had touched her.

"Enough of this!" The priest yelled. "You have been playing with your magic and have conjured up some...thing from the darkness." He eyed her warily. "You need to learn to not mess where we should not be." He scolded her.

Clairance began to become irate. "If you are truly a priest; then how is it, that you do not know of what you speak! I have done nothing to cause darkness to fall here. Movada's form emerged from the darkness! He caused my husband to lay sleeping, undisturbed, while he defiled *my* body!" She screamed at him.

"If you do not know how to help us then leave!" Robbie was also outraged. "Perhaps it is you that have called the darkness upon us." She scorned him and pointed to the door.

The priest looked back at Clairance. He saw the marks and thescratches. He felt the evil coming from them. He had not sensed it since Movada left the castle. He lifted his cross and held it above his head. He muttered a prayer in Latin.-When he opened his eyes, he saw the shadow figure attached to Clairance's body.- He moved forward and pushed the cross into her skin. She screamed in pain. The darkness left her. It swirled around the entire room. Movada's laughter came again. The priest said another prayer. His faith wavered when the darkness came upon him. He fainted.

Balcor raised the Bible up and started reading verses from the book of James. The darkness left the priest and tried to take the book from him.-Balcor held onto it firmly. Hissing and crackling could be heard around the room. Balcor continued to read aloud. Each person said their own prayers to God and the darkness weakened until it had to dissipate.

They breathed deeply and sighed as it lifted. "Thank God." Robbie said when the room was free of him. She checked on her mother and the sleeping priest. They were alive, but shaken. Clairance was staring off into space.-She felt like a different person.

Tinsa, Latell, and Carieve came into the King's office. They were expecting sleepy-looking faces from the night's festivities. Instead, they found gloom and despair.-"What did we miss?" Tinsa asked.

Phoebe flew in with the women. She went to Clairance and sat in her lap. "Are you ok?" She asked. She looked up at her person with a worried expression on her face. "What happened Clair?"

Clairance reached down and stroked Phoebe's hair. She smoothed her little hands on her own. "Dearest. I am better now." Clairance smiled down at her. "Don't you fret."

The fairies came inside to get her. "Come on Phoebe, let's play." Dery was the first to address the room. "Hello everyone." He grabbed her by the hand. "Let's fly." Phoebe giggled and let him lead her out the window.

Ganter came into the study with Revie and Remid. "It's time." He nodded to Kyle. "There has been much amiss. We need to find the remedy."

They had prepared the horses in advance. A large extravagant coach was waiting also, for the duke and the king. Sariah and Robbie begged to go. "No." They were told. "Let men's work be men's work. Attend to Clairance."

The men gathered a small brunch from the kitchen along with canteens. They gathered their weapons just in case they had any unwanted encounters. Ganter led them through the villages and past Camo Forest. Dirt kicked up everywhere from the speed of the horses. The carriage rumbled through and bounced a few times on the rough terrain. They had to make a circle and go around the back side of the woods.

The old crone's cottage was just past the inside barrier of trees. It was hidden with vegetation and covered with various strands of ivy. Smoke was coming from the chimney. Puffs of color were mingling in the smoke mixture. Tapping could be heard from inside.

The men slowly dismounted from their steeds. Balcor and Kyle climbed from the coach. They surveyed the land around them and readied their swords. Ganter led the way to the cottage door. They heard more banging followed by chanting and laughter.

Kyle gave Ganter a questioning look. "How did you come to find this place?" He asked him quietly.

Ganter glanced at Kyle and then held his eyes fixed on the doorway. "I had heard of a way to fix our problem. I did not fret about the how." He told him to, still walking forward. They crouched under the window sill to see what they would be walking into. The old crone was throwing things into a cauldron. It was hanging by itself over a fireplace in the middle of the room. Her short, hooded form circled the pot singing her chant. She moved like a younger woman, that wasn't as plump. The men looked at each other.

"Come in, come in." She shouted to them. "It's rude to peer and peek." She laughed again as the door swung open. Her cackle was almost melodic.

Ganter stood first. "I have been here before." He told her. "Yes. I remember you. A bottle of poison for the ruler." She did not look up or look at him. She was not concerned in the least at their arrival. "Woman, what did you sell me?" He asked her.

She cackled and looked at him. "I sold you what you asked for," was her reply. "Were you not satisfied?" She raised an eyebrow and stopped her toiling.

Kyle came forward. "Woman. I am the King of Whispershire. Your potion killed Movada in body only. His spirit demon is raising havoc with us.".- He was becoming angry and frustrated with her banter.

She moved swiftly to him. One second, she was at her cauldron, and the next she was at his feet. She gazed up at him. Her eyes were ablaze and had swirling irises. "King of Whispershire," she whispered. She went around Kyle, studying him. "Yes. Yes. You are the heir."

Kyle nodded. "I am the son of Rosecco and Zipurda," he told her. She laughed at his response.

"Of course, you are!" She exclaimed. "I said you are the heir. I am not blind." She snapped. The hood came off from her cape revealing silver hair. It was disheveled and messy. Her large bosom heaved as she spoke.

"That is not why we are here." Ganter interrupted. "Please, we have a real problem." he said again.

The old crone looked at him moving away from Kyle. Her movements toward Ganter were more reptilian. She hissed at him and licked her teeth. "You got what you came for. You asked for poison to kill him. You said no one would ever want to see his face again." She scanned his body for movements that may be a threat.

Ganter swallowed and nodded his head. "Yes ma'am. I did. But it didn't work. We see his face in his apparitions! He manifests himself and we hear him!" Ganter tried to maintain control over his fear and anger.

"Lady. We did not come here to start a fight." Balcor stated diplomatically, entering the cottage with Revie and Remid coming to his side. She seemed oddly familiar to him.

She looked at Balcor and raised an eyebrow. "No. Duke Balcor. You brought your body-guards to witness me at work." She cackled again. Balcor took a step back. "How do you know me?"

The old crone looked him over. "You are brother to Rosecco. King Kyle's uncle." She bowed and laughed. "Do not mock me in my own home!"

Balcor nodded. "I meant no offense. I know magic has a way to see all. You are aged and wise. I only meant to ask if we had ever met before?"

"Hmmmm." She made a few other noises as well. "Officially. No." She nodded in agreement with her answer. "I never lie." She raised her eyebrows at him, silently asking him if he was going to rebuff her answer.

Balcor smiled. "Neither do I."-He leaned forward as he said it. "How do I know you?" He thought to himself, studying her manner. Kyle took in a deep breath that was audible in the small room. There seemed to be an echo surrounding the inside of the cottage. Revie and Remid sucked in air through their teeth as well.

"Is there anything that you can do to help us be rid of this demon ghost?" Kyle asked. Tenger came up to stand next to him, and he nodded. The crone turned toward him, then to her cauldron. Her eyes rolled to the back of her head. She leaned into her pot. "Potio, potio, videam! Daemonium sanguinem."- She leaned two and fro, saying the chant into her crock. "Comprime venenum!" When she accentuated the last word, the pot shook and spun. Blue smoke rose from it, followed by red. The old crone grabbed a dropper and bottle.

She ladled the contents into the bottle and placed the topper on it. She turned and faced Kyle. "What is it worth to ye?" She asked him. Kyle looked at his clothing and found a few coins in his pocket. He tossed the silver to her. She laughed in response. "What do I need of money for?"- She laughed again.-"What is it worth?" She asked again.

"I do not understand. Be plain woman. What do you want for it?" Kyle asked her.

"Think." She hissed. "I want to know what it is worth to ye." She rocked back and forth. Her eyes changed colors. Dust formed in her hand. She threw it into the pot. It exploded with orange and green flames. "Next will be the vial which contains your cure." She threatened them.

Kyle thought. "I can offer you anything you desire. It is worth much to me. Movada killed my father. He threw my mother out to die. He slaughtered my friends and family. He took over the throne and enslaved the people. His demon is harassing my wife, and as of last night, raped her mother!" He shook his head. "Please! What do you want for it?"

The woman became outraged. "This demon assaulted Clairance!?!" She shook and grew taller. She breathed as if she would spit fire. "I will come and kill him myself!" She wrapped her cloak around her and disappeared with the vile.

The men looked at each other. Ganter shook his head. "I am sorry, my liege." He said to Kyle and Balcor.-"I have done this to us. I will fix it." He ran from the cottage and jumped onto his horse. The men followed his lead.

The horses ran faster away from the cottage than they had run to get there. The men were mortified and confused at what had transpired there. This old crone was a witch. She had made a potion to kill the demon. She knew them. She knew their families. "But how?" It was what they all were thinking about.- "What is her relationship to Clairance?"-Kyle said aloud.

Balcor shook his head bewildered also. "I couldn't say." He thought for a moment. "Kasde was in the forest, and so was Villae. They were to protect Robbie in her transition. They have magic in their veins. At the mention of Clairance. The witch became outraged." He shook his head again. "This is a different part of the forest. There were no other enchantments other than her spells. None that I saw, anyway."

Kyle nodded in understanding, seeing his angle. "She must be family." The men nodded their agreement with this realization. "That is the only explanation for what happened there." The men sat silently for the rest of
the journey. They had made a day and a half's journey in a day. They stopped to rest at Vole Tirfs.

Balcor's servants brought them refreshments as they entered. Another of the stable boys came to gather the horses. Revie and Remid retreated to their quarters. Ganter came to the guest's lodging area and stood against the wall. He no longer had a room here. Tenger stood next to him. "So, you and Tinsa, huh?" he started a conversation.

Ganter laughed, looking Tenger over. "Yes." He smiled and stared at the floor, imagining her beauty. "It is nice to meet you and your fiancé. Tinsa speaks highly of all of her friends." He said when he looked up.

Tenger shrugged his shoulders and started to play with his goatee. "It has been an adventure." He winked at him. "Have you broken with her father yet?" Tenger asked.

Ganter flashed him a look of shock and surprise. "No. I hadn't thought that far ahead, honestly." Ganter laughed awkwardly.

Tenger laughed again. "It's not the end of the world to be engaged to a beautiful woman." He cast Ganter a side-eyed look. Kyle and Balcor walked past them heading to Balcor's study. They were lost in thought about the old crone and the new potion. They need to figure out her plan. Tenger and Ganter followed them unaware of their new found truths.

Balcor sat at the head of his small table. Kyle sat to his right. They discussed the possibilities of what the crone would do. They did not know exactly what she said to make her potion, or how she was to use it against him. "All of this magical stuff is new to me." Kyle stated. "I have never used a potion or a spell. I am still getting used to the idea of a courtyard full of fairies!" He exclaimed.

"I have seen a thing or two in my time." Balcor told them. "I have not seen it directly, but I have heard rumors of it." Balcor unconsciously twiddled his thumbs. "What do we know for certain?"

Kyle creased his eyebrows. He played with the ring on his finger. "I have a wife and mother-in-law that wield healing powers."

He said thoughtfully. "Robbie's aunt is a witch."- Kyle sighed and scratched his head.

"There is more than one type of magic." Tenger added. "I have only seen Robbie's family use their powers for good. Movada is definitely of another sort."

"Robbie used the word "demonic" to describe it." Kyle told them. "The dark arts are not something that we are accustomed to."

Tenger took a seat next to Kyle. "What did the old crone say to make her potion? How is it used?" He asked. "Was that dark magic also?" "Maybe you need dark magic to thwart dark magic?" Ganter stated a question sitting next to Balcor.

"We believe the old crone to be family to Clairance." Balcor told the other men who were not in the carriage. "If they are good, then so is she." Balcor shook his head.

Ganter sighed. The men looked at each other perplexed. "He had to drink the poison. What is she going to do against a ghost?" Ganter asked after a few minutes of silence.

Balcor looked to a distant place on the wall of his chamber. He stood and walked toward a picture. He studied the portrait for a moment, and then took it off the wall, carefully placing it on the floor. Behind the picture was a cloth that covered a safely hidden hole in the wall. Balcor looked at the men. "No one speaks of this." He told them.

They all watched as Balcor removed the cloth. He reached inside the hiding hole and brought forth a glowing dagger. "I have heard a reference to this as an angel blade." He brought the dagger back to the table and laid it flat in the middle. The men didn't dare touch it. They stared at it bewildered.

Each man careened his neck to further inspect the blade. The handle was made of brass and had a ceramic blade. There were different jewels encrusted in it. Each one had been placed intricately in a pattern that resembled the stars. Tenger scratched his head. "I have heard of this. I have never seen it. It is known to be a demon slayer."

Balcor placed it in the cloth and carefully wrapped it. "Aye." He spoke. "A woman gave it to me a long time ago. I didn't know her. I was questioning it then. She said it would be needed in the future." He took a deep breath. "I placed it in the wall, so it wouldn't come into dangerous hands. I had forgotten all about it until now."

Balcor placed the wrapped weapon into his cloak. "We need to get to Whispershire." He placed his hands on the table. "If everyone is ready, we will go." Balcor walked from the room with the men not far behind him. Ganter ran to retrieve Remid and Revie. They nodded and followed.

The men were once again on the road. There was no way to beat the old woman there. "What did you give her for the poison?" Revie asked Ganter.

Ganter frowned. "I told her that I was merely a servant. There wasn't much value that she could get from me." He sighed as if embarrassed. "What did you give her?" Tenger asked him again, more forcefully.

Ganter bowed his head and whispered "An orgasm."

The men laughed hysterically. "What did you do?" Remid asked. "How could you keep an erection looking at that?" He laughed. Ganter swallowed. "I don't want to talk about it."-He fell behind the men as they laughed at him. At least, he knew he could please Tinsa when the time came, he thought to himself. That thought made him smile. He quickened the pace of his horse. He smiled nonchalantly. The men gave each other worried glances as they kept pace with the carriage. They arrived at Whispershire the next afternoon. They were famished and tired. Servants rushed out to meet them bearing water canteens and bread.

Nothing was amiss. There was melancholy throughout the castle. Balcor was baffled by it. It had been not even three days since the time their unwanted visitor had been there. How were they not still in an uproar? Balcor swiftly walked to his chamber.

Kyle rushed upstairs to find Robbie. "We are back." He said walking into the room. He found Robbie sound asleep in their bed. He sat next to her. He smoothed the hair from her forehead and kissed it lightly.

Her blue eyes fluttered open and she smiled up at him. "Hello." She breathed. Her head turned on the pillow as she adjusted to make room for her husband.

He removed his tunic and boots. He lay next to her wrapping his arm around her stomach. "How are you, my love?" he asked. "I'm sleeping." She replied dreamily.

Kyle kissed the back of her neck and let her sleep peacefully. He would get a full report after a nap. He drifted off to sleep next to his beautiful wife.

Ganter, Tenger, Remind, and Revie went straight to the kitchen. They grabbed what they could find under sackcloth and on hanging racks. They poured some milk and ate confections. Rested, and their hunger satisfied, they went to find their ladies.

CHAPTER ELEVEN

Clairance sat in a chair in her bed chamber. She was knitting a blanket, for the new babe that she had seen coming in her dreams. She smiled to herself with her secret. Kasde had joined the men in the fields. Phoebe came and looked after her from time to time. They knew that evil had been upon them. Clairance tried to not think of it or pay it any heed. She was past her child bearing years. It had done nothing other than wound her pride.

Kasde had told her that "It didn't matter. It wasn't her choosing to sleep with another. Movada had forced his way into their room and he would pay for it." They weren't sure how. Clairance tried to keep her eyes and mind on the future. She had everything she needed right in front of her. Villae was even not that far away, taking care of their old home.

Villae popped in now and again as well. Clairance had not welcomed her magic like Villae had. She had wanted a normal life with her husband and daughter. Their mother was not impressed. She had taken off to live somewhere else. Clairance hadn't thought of her in years. She wondered how the memory of her mom had come to her out of the blue.

Her head hurt. She rubbed her temples, and then she saw a flash of light. The room began to spin around her. Her mother appeared from out of nowhere. "Clairance!" She cried. She ran to hold her.

"Mother?" Clairance questioned her arrival. "What are you doing here?" Clairance took in her mother's haggard appearance. The black, hooded cloak hung around her shoulders. Her hair had turned silver in color since the last time that she had seen her. She had also put on a few pounds.

"Your son-in-law just came to see me." She told her. She shook the vile at her. "You should've come yourself." She scolded. "What has happened here?" She demanded.

"You have no right to just pop in after all of these years and demand answers. You abandoned us!" Clairance exclaimed.

"I had to. Your sister took over my cave!" She answered defiantly. "You never came back. You wanted" she lowered her voice and mocked the word "love."

"You can leave now." Clairance told her flatly. She picked up her knitting needles and started to rush her fingers.

"No. I cannot." Her mother defended. "You have been taken advantage of by a demon!" She was outraged. "You should've been strong enough to stop it. But no, you refused to use your magic. Didn't you?"

Clairance glared at her mother. "I tried. He was too strong. He was already dead and buried!" Tears stung her eyes.

Eleana hurried to her daughter's side. She wrapped her arms around Clairance's head. "Hush now. It's over. Mother's here."-She cooed into her ear and rocked her like a child, sitting on the edge of the chair. "I have a potion to kill the demon." She told her matter-of-factly when the tears stopped.

"I should have known that you provided the poison." Clairance laughed. "What did you take from Ganter? His soul?"

Eleana laughed. "No, no, something much less significant." She smiled mischievously at her daughter, and winked.

"Ugh, Mother!" Clairance was disgusted.

"It had been a very long time since a man had come to me, alone." She informed her. "Besides you have yours now, whenever you want him." Clairance gave her mother a disgusted look, then she smiled and rolled her eyes. "Poor Ganter." She laughed.

"I didn't screw him like this! I made myself beautiful to him. I am not a savage!" She laughed back.

Just then, Villae joined them. "What the hell?"

"Hello daughter." Eleana said.

"Mother." Villae raised her eyebrows and looked at her sister. "Clairance, what on earth?"

Clairance rolled her eyes. She took a deep breath and sighed. She explained what happened a few days earlier. They were both dumbstruck at how it could have happened to one of them. "I told you. This demon is strong. He was magical himself, before his death. Now it's like magical poison gives him more power."

Villae shook her head at her mother. "Didn't you get all of the facts?"

Eleana stared ahead. A scowl crept onto her face. "I didn't know that he had anything to do with magic, other than just being an evil being." She stared at the floor. "This will have to be remedied. I only made a potion to slay a monster. Not a magical being that had been removed from his body." She stamped her foot and walked around Clairance's room.

Villae watched her mother's rant. "I can't believe you did this!" She breathed out vehemently. "You had better come up with a solution on how to fix it!" She threw her hands around angrily.

"I know!" Eleana shouted.

The shouting woke Robbie and Kyle. They knocked loudly. "What's going on in there? Is everything ok?" Kyle demanded.

"Shit!" Eleana swore. "Now, look what you've done!"

Kyle burst through the door at her outburst. He looked around the room and saw the old crone. "You!" He pointed at her.

She growled. "And you!" She made a face. "Don't point at me!" She shook her head and hissed something toward him.

"Don't you dare curse my son!" Clairance blocked it. "Damn you Mother!" She yelled standing.

"Curse!" Kyle exclaimed.

"Mother!" Robbie shouted.

They all looked around the room at each other. Every one of them was fuming. Villae laughed when she saw how everyone was huffing. "Well, it looks as if you have quite a bit of explaining to do." She laughed again, glancing from her mother to her sister. She twirled her cloak around her and spun, disappearing.

Robbie stomped her foot. "What the hell is going on?" She demanded. She stared at her mother and then at her grandmother! She sent a side eyed glance to her husband who seemed to know. She looked from one to the next and demanded answers.

Kyle looked at Robbie. "Balcor and I figured it out on the way here." He shrugged his shoulders. "I would've said something but you were sleeping so sweetly."

"Balcor!" Eleana shouted.

"Figured out that I have a grandmother!?" Robbie asked incredulously. She threw her hands into the air. "What else is a big secret with this family?" She yelled at them.

"Get Balcor in here." Eleana commanded them, ignoring Robbie.

Robbie glared at her. "How are *you*, my grandmother? Where have you been all my life?" She turned to her mother. "How do I have a grandmother I didn't know about? What else are you hiding from me?" She yelled at them.

Eleana glared at Robbie. "Calm down, child." She waved her hand to hush her. "Your questions are trivial, at best. We have more important things to attend to here." She looked at Kyle and raised her eyebrow.

"Get Balcor." Kyle sighed and left the room. He walked hastily down the hall to Balcor's chambers. Kyle knocked softly at first. He didn't want to disturb his uncle. There was something more pressing to figure out.

He knocked louder. "Who's there?" Balcor demanded.

"It's me. We need your assistance. The old crone is here. She's asking for you." Kyle said through the closed door. He listened for a response. There were noises coming from inside like the throwing of a shoe. Balcor came to the door.

He was half dressed, buttoning his shirt as he opened it. "This better be important." Balcor stated. He glared at his nephew for interrupting his time with his wife. He let out a slow, labored breath. "Where is she?"

Kyle stepped back and let him out. Balcor closed the door behind him, to keep his wife's integrity intact, as she was covering her nakedness. "She is in Clairance's room. " Kyle informed him.

Balcor didn't seem surprised. He let out another puff of air as he followed Kyle back up the long hallway. "What does she want with me?" He asked.

"I don't know, Uncle." Kyle replied. Once at the door Kyle tapped on it lightly, then walked through it. The women were sitting in the bedroom in silence. Kyle looked at them all to see who would be the first to say something.

"What is the meaning of this?" Balcor asked. "What is your business with me?" He stared down Eleana.

Eleana pushed her cloak back over her head. Her silver hair hung loosely around her shoulders and down her back. She used an age reversal spell to make herself appear younger.

Balcor gasped. He swallowed the lump that formed in his throat. Balcor looked at Kyle with a surprised look on his face. He then turned his attention back to Eleana. "Well then," Balcor said. "That explains that." He shook his head in disbelief.

Kyle looked at Balcor. "Explains what?" He was confused, as were Clairance and Robbie.

Balcor cleared his throat. "She gave me the angel blade." He bowed his head to her. Balcor thought for a moment. "Woman, explain yourself." He said observing her.

Eleana made the spell vanish. "Balcor, I know you from long ago." She started to tell them. "I found the blade as I made my way through the forest to my new home. As you clever gentlemen have discovered, I am Clairance's mother." She looked at her daughter. "My family has always had special gifts, well, that make us outcast.

Different." She was looking at Kyle as she spoke. She turned her attention back to Clairance, and Robbie.

"Clairance didn't want her gifts. She wanted a normal life. I let her try. It broke my heart that she didn't want to stay with me. Villae took her magic in stride. She became very powerful. She kicked me out of my own home! I moved to the other side of the forest." She gave her daughter a sorrowful look. "A demon came and took their father from me. My unique gifts led me to the angel blade. I used it against the demon, but he took my husband with him to Hell." Eleana became irritable with the memory that she had tried to forget. She sighed and turned to Robbie.

"The only way to get in touch with our ancestors, and receive our gifts, was through the forest, and the fairy magic." Eleana took a deep breath. "That is why Robbie had to enter, and remain for long enough to know her history. Those fairies led them right to Villae's dwelling. Right to her father, as I'm sure that is why he let them out." She sent a side glance to her daughter. "Robbie has only to choose a path. She can live a life like Clairance did. Or she can embrace her gifts."

She looked at Robbie with grief in her eyes. "You did not remain in the forest long enough for an explanation. I do believe that you would've chosen Kyle anyway." Eleana sighed.

"Of course, I did! Kyle was wounded. He needed me!" Robbie exclaimed, standing. She moved next to her husband, and stood by his side. She put a possessive arm around his waist.

Eleana sighed. "As well you should have." She nodded her head. "But you didn't get your history or learn to use your gifts." She shook her head at them.

"What does this have to do with me?" Balcor asked again.

"Balcor. I knew of your family. I saw a vision that you would need the blade. I did not know when or why. I do now." She looked Balcor in the eyes. "I gave Ganter a poison to kill the body of a man. That is what he asked for. Movada was a dark warlock from another place. I did not know Ganter's target. I also did not know that Movada had powers." She sat in the chair that Robbie had just vacated. Eleana took a deep breath. "We have unleashed the demon." She nodded to herself. "It needs to be killed again. And it needs to be killed for good."

"How are we supposed to do that?" Kyle asked. "He has no body," He paused, looking at Clairance. "Unless he wants one."

"Exactly." Eleana answered.

Kyle scratched his head. "I don't understand." He shook his hands out and took a deep breath.

"We must resurrect the body. Then we join the demon with it. We must kill the soul of a powerful being, and send it back to hell." Eleana knew what they had to do.

"How?" Clairance asked.

"That is where the problem lies." Eleana answered. "This one is very strong. He is probably an ancient force. That is why we need our combined magic, and the angel blade."

They all looked around the room at each other. Robbie shook her head. "This is crazy!" She exclaimed. "It would get us all killed!" She looked at her husband.

"Where is the body?" Eleana asked.

"It is at Vole Tirfs." Balcor answered skeptically.

"And the blade, where is it?" She asked again.

Balcor stared at her. "It is in my room."

Robbie gasped. Clairance stared at Balcor. "How did I not know about this?" Clairance asked. She looked at her mother and then at Balcor. She swallowed. "I have not used my magic other than to heal. Robbie also. How do you expect us to join yours?" She asked.

"You need to practice. You need Villae." Eleana answered, again nodding to them. "Both of you."

Kyle shook his head. "Practice what? Where?" He probed.

110

Eleana glared at him. "You have known these people your whole life. Have you never noticed something extra about them?" She creased her brows, and frowned. "Balcor, you also. Even Zipurda knew of magic and transformation. How can you not have opened your eyes?"

"My mother!?" Kyle asked, doubting his ears.

"There are more around here than you know. Think." Eleana told them. "Who else is here that we can use?"

Clairance thought for a moment and mentioned Robbie's friends. "Tinsa, Tenger, and Nelame have gifts. I have seen them." Clairance suggested. Robbie's mouth dropped open. Clairance looked at her daughter. "How do you think you have been drawn to them? Either they have magic in them or around them."

"Robbie, go get your friends." Eleana told her. "Balcor get the blade, and find out how to use it. Kyle, take men and go back to Vole Tirfs," She squinted her eyes. "Retrieve that body." Eleana took charge. "Clairance, I need you to make amends with your sister and find a way to raise the dead."

Eleana thought for a moment and stood. "I need to make another potion, and find a way to lure him out."

Kyle asked everyone that wasn't necessary, to leave the castle. He wanted to make sure that the people were safe. Eleana and Clairance were going to turn the castle gardens into a school of magic. They had to convince Villae first.

"This isn't my fight! I had nothing to do with it!" Villae screeched to them. "Why should I help this place that doesn't believe?" She became indignant and threw her hands around as she spoke.

"Villae. You are the most powerful witch that we know. We know also that you like to be in charge. Are you saying that you wouldn't?" Eleana played into her emotional head game.

Villae huffed. She placed her hands on her hips. "I have earned my status and to be alone if I want to. I don't need to teach a

111

bunch of bratty, humanoid children, barely out of their teens, how to use magic." She huffed again. "There is not enough time in the world to show them how to use it properly! Especially when they have no idea what it is that they possess!" She glared at her mother and sister.

Clairance sent a wave of relaxation through the room. The blue light was barely visible on the floor as she sent it to her sister's feet. Eleana saw her and smiled. She added her magic to it. She sent a pink wave of persuasion, and reason.

Villae changed her attitude completely. She smiled. "I'm so happy that you are here. I have missed you both." She said. She folded her skirt over itself and sat down at the kitchen table. "Who are these kids?" She asked.

Robbie smiled. "Tinsa, from the village market. Her eyes can cast shadows, and change routes. She has the ability to make plans, and make everyone happy. She also has superior intellect. Nelame, my other friend, has power over plants and animals. She can help things grow and talk to creatures. Tenger is her fiancé. He actually looks the part. He has the strength of several men. He has persuasive powers. They have used their gifts but have not known that it was actually magical."

"There are also a few volunteers from the villages. They think that they might come in handy." Clairance added, also smiling. She gave her mother a side eyed smirk.

Robbie leaned her elbows on the table. "These are hardly teenagers. We are all at least twenty." Robbie giggled. "Thank you Villae. Your efforts will be greatly appreciated." She smiled at her aunt, her blue eyes shining.

Villae shook her head. "I must be crazy."

Eleana laughed. "Whatever would give you that idea?"

Villae searched around her cottage with her eyes. She glared at them when she saw the magical aura fading from the floor. "I'm not crazy! You are! How dare you get me to agree, using magic against me!" She stood and swooshed her hands. The door opened.

"Get out of here! All three of you!" She flung her hands toward the door swooshing them back.

"Villae! Wait!" Clairance exclaimed.

"No. Shut up and get out!" Villae snorted. "I'll be there when I get there. Now get lost!" She closed the door in their faces with a flip of her hands.

Robbie smiled at her mother and grandmother. They walked back to the castle. They had already sent messengers to the village, for the others to come to the castle. Kyle was preparing the grounds when they arrived. The gardens were transformed. He had placed large white, canvas tents, and wooden tables around the yards. He wasn't sure what they would need. Kyle kept the kitchen staff at the castle, as well as a few others, to help with sanitation and meals.

"Thank you, Kyle." Clairance told him when they saw it.

"I don't know what else you will need." Kyle stated, scratching his head. "Just let me know, I guess."

Robbie walked swiftly to him. She kissed him on the cheek. "It's perfect."

Tenger and Nelame entered the garden right after the women did. "Looks like an old-fashioned camp out to me." Tenger said laughing to his fiancé.

Nelame cast him a knowing look. She smiled and rolled her eyes. She hugged Robbie and picked a tent for her belongings. Tenger followed suit as did Tinsa entering the garden. Eleana nodded her agreement with their decisions.

The fairies came out from their hiding places. They began making the tents colorful and covered in flowers and greenery. Birds came and sang to them as they toiled. Their songs were repeated back to them by the fairies. The entire garden became peacefully serene. Small white flowers drifted in the breeze. There was not a cloud in sight. Blue skies covered them and them and the sun shone brightly. Hammocks were strewn up between the trees that were close enough together. The tents had gossamer sheets covering the front, tied back with string. One large tent was for the women and another for the men. Robbie and Kyle would stay in their room as would Clairance and Kasde.

Kasde walked forward with Villae on his arm. They entered the garden from the eastern gate, that was closer to the fields. Villae had invited him to help instruct. Kasde had a way with small minds. They fairies adored him. He answered their childish questions with ease, in a way that they could understand. Villae huffed at the tents. She lowered her eyes to the grounds. With a wave of her hand across her body, she thrust down a mat to sit on.

Kyle had lunch brought out to them. They talked and laughed with each other as they ate. They had not sat down as friends since before Kyle and Robbie had become royalty. The mood was jovial.

Villae had finished with her dinner first. She studied the faces around her. She watched for any signs that they would be any use to them. She watched how they moved and carried themselves. Villae raised her eyebrows. She looked at her sister who was sitting happily with her husband. She also watched Robbie with Kyle and Tenger with Nelame. She and Tinsa sat alone. Tinsa wasn't bothered by it, but someone was special to her as well.

Other villagers came in during the luncheon. A woman in her forties and two men in their thirties. They all knew each other and seemed to be at ease in one another's company. Villae sneered at the new woman. She was dainty and small. She looked no one in the eyes. Her clothing seemed to be her leisure wear. This woman wore breeches like the men. She was peculiar. The villagers called her Kat. The men were engaging with each other and laughing about something off from the others. They were William and John.

Warg came outside to see what the noises were about. He was trying to enjoy the sunshine on the other side of the garden. "What's this then?" He asked, coming to them.

"I said to leave the castle, for your safety." Kyle told him standing. He walked toward Warg. The others watched to see how the new king would handle disobedience. Kyle hugged him tightly and wrapped his arm around his side. Kyle led him back to his quarters. "Why are you here?" He asked him.

"I have never left. I stayed through your fathers rule and your mother's disappearance. I stayed through Movada and I will stay now too." Warg told him.

Kyle sighed and looked at him with sadness. "I am sorry everything has happened in your stay here at the castle. I am glad of it too. I love you, old man." Kyle told him. He laughed.

Warg chuckled warmly. "I love you too, son." He sat on his bed when they returned to his chamber. "I might watch from my window if that is alright with you?"

Kyle nodded and laughed. "You will do as you please, anyway." He sighed. "Please be cautious. They will be learning how to use magic!" Kyle's eyes widened and he used a hand gesture as he spoke the last word. Kyle laughed again. "You need to rest. You have been out a lot lately." Kyle told him.

Warg smiled. "Yes, your majesty." He chuckled.

Kyle gave him a sideways glance before closing the door behind him. He shook his head as he retreated from the castle. Entering the garden from the other side, he saw the people gathering together. Kyle sat on the bench and watched from afar.

Robbie moved gracefully as she moved her arms to gather energy. She closed her eyes and swayed. She didn't mean to be, but her movements were seductive and genuine. Kyle smiled watching her. A ball of light appeared in her hands. She opened her eyes. Villae tossed a target of some sort into the sky. Robbie threw the ball into the air and made the target explode.

The gathering cheered. "Faster." Villae instructed. "Focus." She tapped the ground with a stick. Nelame stood next. Villae told her to concentrate on her gifts and pull energy from the earth. Nelame closed her eyes and tried to focus like Robbie did. Vines appeared around her arms and laced around to her fingertips. "Throw it. Wrap someone in it. Do something with your gift!" Villae shouted to her.

Nelame tried to focus. She pushed the vines from her hands. Flowers blossomed around her. Her body shook from the force. She shook her head and sat down. "I'm sorry." She said.

Villae guffawed. "Ugh." She said. She glared at Nelame for a moment. "How about we get you to use it to harm an enemy. What would make you want to?" She looked at Tenger and raised her eyebrow. She moved her fingers at him and lifted him from the ground. She made his body tense and stretch out in all directions, just enough to make him yelp in pain. Nelame tensed.

"Well, are you going to save him, before I tear his limbs off?" Villae harassed her. She tightened her hold on Tenger. He groaned audibly. Nelame became infuriated and frightened. She pulled harder from the earth and the rocks. She closed her eyes tightly. She grew the vines and sent them sailing around her lover. She pulled him back to her as Villae released her hold.

"Hmmmm, better." Villae told her. Nelame held Tenger in her arms and tried to comfort him, asking him if he was ok. "He's fine." Villae told her laughing. "He's here for his strength is he not?" She mocked them.

William went next. "I don't know what gifts that I have. I just wanted to help." He said. Villae studied him. He was average height and weight. He had muscular arms and legs, strawberry blonde hair and green eyes. Villae circled him. She pulled her senses to find something about him that she could use. "I see artistic sight in you. Go work with the fairies." She told him.

John stood for his inspection. "I have also never used magic." He told her. Villae circled him. He was darker than the other men, with brown eyes and black hair. He also seemed to be the average merchant. There was something about him that impressed on her senses but she wasn't sure what it was yet. Villae raised an eyebrow at him. She sighed. "Sit back down. I will get to you later."

Villae went next to Kat and passed her by. "Tinsa. Your turn." She said. Tinsa raised her silver-gray eyes to her and nodded as she stood. She licked her lips and began singing a hymnal tune. Her eyes changed color as she pulled magic to her, the way that her friends had. She imagined a different place and time. The surroundings changed. They were now sitting around a water fountain ornamented with cherubs. She pushed her magic to them, and the crowd began laughing as if they were intoxicated. Tinsa stopped singing and the garden went back to the way it was.

Villae smiled. "Very good." She complimented her and smiled her approval. She looked at Clairance who was also smiling at Tinsa, while holding hands with Kasde. Robbie was excited to see her friends' power. Then there was Kat. She stood. Kat pulled crystals from her pockets and threw them on the ground. She reached into her shirt and brought out another crystal on a necklace. She rubbed it. The crystal glowed with heat. Kat's hair stood on end. The crystals around her formed the shape of a circle around her. She willed the energy from the crystals to move. She pointed her necklace toward a faraway tree. It crackled and burst into flames.

Villae nodded and smiled. "Now that we can use!" She became excited. She smiled and wiggled her eyebrows at Clairance. "Very good." Villae waved her hand in the air. Candles appeared on the tables. She flicked her teeth with her tongue and snapped her fingers. The candles ignited. Villae waved her arm in the air and the flames extinguished. Clairance sent a wave of energy to the tree that was ablaze. It also dowsed its flames.

Nelame sent growing energy to it as Robbie engaged her magic with Nelame's to heal the tree. The tree popped and shed its burnt particles. Green sprouts came forth and grew. Tinsa sent the tree water. The tree became full grown and sprouted leaves and shade. Robbie and Nelame smiled at each other and dropped their hands. Tinsa also was content with their work.

"Bravo." Kasde piped up. "Working together for a common use is why we are here. Well done." He beamed at his daughter. They all stared at Kat.

"Where are you from?" Clairance asked her. "I have not seen you around here before."

Kat stood silent. She thrust her hands into her pockets and sighed. When she spoke, it was in a different language than any of them had heard before. John came forward to translate. He had found his purpose.

She spoke of a place across the sea. No one believed it. She did have quite a different look to her. Besides the awkward wardrobe, she had long ebony hair in small braids. Her skin was also a bit darker than the rest, and dark brown eyes. She and John could've been mistaken for brother and sister.

"No matter." Kasde said. "We are all brought together here. We thank you all for offering your services."

"We are going up against a demon with magic. You will not be fighting targets or trees." Villae told them walking in a circle around the camp. "This villain will fight back. He is ruthless. He will not show mercy. We do not know the extent of his powers." She warned them. "You will fight against each other. Get used to someone hurting from your powers and get used to them hurting you. We do have two healers amongst us." She looked them all in the eye, individually as she circled again. "Your training starts now!"

William was learning from the fairies, how to make what he saw in his head. He could create mirages and holograms. Eleana nodded and went off to find spells and herbs. She gathered verbena, rue, rosemary, sage, thyme, clovers, myrrh and angelica. There was also henbane, wolfbane, mugwart, and different strands of mint. Eleana needed leaves to wrap it in and a fire pit to make her potions.

Eleana chose a tent for meditation. She sat cross legged on the tent floor. She closed her eyes and chanted a mantra to herself. She accessed her mental portal to the ancestors. She tapped into the olden

118

spell books. Her eyes rolled back in her head as she read through them.

Incantations could be tricky. They had to be done just right, to achieve the desired result. She had to get the pronunciation down to a T. The spells also had to be done in order to make the right potions. This was a complicated task. It had to be attended to delicately. Eleana would also need to go into the forest, and find the right ingredients to make her magic work; animal parts. With all of the information that she needed she broke her trans. Walking out of the tent she said "I'll be needing a horse."

She looked at Kyle, who was on the far bench. He had sent away the stable hands. Kyle laughed and got up. "Right away." He told her. "Where are you going?" Kyle saddled Ablom for her. With the new knowledge, he guessed that Robbie's horse knew the way. She would be a good steed anyway for someone who hasn't rode in a while. Eleana didn't want to use her magic up by transporting there and back. They needed all of their strength for the fight against Movada's demon.

Eleana rode Ablom hard and fast. She accompanied the men to Vole Tirfs, and then went out on her own after that. Balcor's lands were a little further than halfway to the forest. Kyle, Tenger, Kasde, and Ganter went into the duke's house.

It was going to be an interesting conversation with the staff. Revie and Remid greeted them at the gate. "What's going on?" They asked.

Kyle got off from his horse. He led the way toward the castle. Kyle placed his arm around Revie's shoulders as they walked. "We need to extract the body of our enemy."

Revie froze. "What!?" He exclaimed with shock. "No way!" He turned and looked at the rest of the men that nodded. That is what they were here to do.

Remid came forward to Kyle's side. "What for?" He creased his brows in worry. "We have put a monster down. You want his body for a trophy?" He asked.

Kyle laughed awkwardly. "Not exactly."

Ganter was fidgeting with his fingers. This was his fault. He ordered the poison to go. He had known that Movada had powers when he gave him the bottle. He just didn't know that it mattered. Ganter moved past the men, brushing the shoulder of Revie as he did so.

"Hey, what's your problem?" Revie asked him as he shrugged it off. He followed Ganter's movements into the castle. Revie looked back at Tenger who shrugged.

"It is important that we take the body back to Whispershire. We do have some haste." Kasde informed them.

Remid and Revie were baffled. They looked at each other and then followed Ganter. Ganter was searching for something in his old quarters. He wouldn't say what. Movada's body was laid in the ground just outside the back courtyards. Kyle instructed the men in the stables to get shovels.

Each one gave him a look of guardedness. "Sire?"

"Get shovels!" He commanded them again. Kyle was already weary of their task. He was being questioned left and right. It was making him act irrationally irritable. Kyle was pacing back and forth.

"Calm down, get it together man!" Tenger told him, slapping him on the back. He walked past Kyle and headed to the back court. "What are we transporting this thing on?" He asked.

Kyle creased his brow again. He hadn't thought of that. It may cause alarm if they just throw a dirt covered body over a horse, and ride through the villages.

Revie said "We have a sling of sorts and some hunting cloth."

Remid agreed. "We could wrap him up like meat and drag him on the sling sled." He shook his head at the thought, but it should work.

Kyle nodded in agreement. Revie and Remid went to retrieve the sled and the things that were needed. Ganter came forward with some tying rope. "This will do nicely." He stated. Kyle drew in a deep breath. He walked past the kitchen and helped himself to a piece of bread and some goat's milk. He huffed and then went out back.

Remid and Revie were tying the sled to Tenger's horse. The stable boys were standing by, with the shovels that were requested. Kyle went to the grave and spit on it. Kasde did the same. They kicked at the dirt with their boots.

"What are you all waiting for?" Kyle shouted. "Get this waste of space out of the ground!" He stomped around to the other side. Tears welled in his eyes. Angry strides mocked the feelings that couldn't be expressed. He breathed heavily.

The sound of dirt being thrown and shovels digging rang in his ears. Kyle fell to his knees and let out a loud scream. Kasde placed his hand on Kyle's shoulder. A tear rolled down his face. He felt the emotions of his son-in-law, and then some. He was furious about what this monster had done to his wife.

"Get it together." Tenger came to them.

"He's right." Ganter added. "This is just the beginning." Shovels continued to dig and toss dirt to the side. With each strike Kyle felt it tugging. His heart beat matched their strikes to the ground. His fury and torment were unquenchable. Kyle squeezed his eyes shut and stood. Kasde remained behind him for support.

The horse neighed. The startled men jumped. The air around them was thick with panic. Each shovel full of soil removed was closer to the evil thing beneath. The thud of metal hitting wood stopped them. The silence was deafening. Bile rose in their throats as the shovel hit the coffin. The men shivered from the task at hand. They swallowed, and closed their eyes. A few of them said a prayer.

"Keep digging, men. We need to be able to get that thing up here." Tenger took control of the situation. He took a shovel from one of the men and began to dig around the cheap wooden box. Tenger threw twice as much dirt as the others. He reached down for a handle. Tenger grunted and lifted the coffin up on one end.

Ganter threw down a rope. Tenger tied it around the coffin, and then through the handle, before throwing the other side back up. Revie caught it and tied it to the horse. Remid led the horse forward. The coffin creaked and groaned before it started to move slowly upward. There was an audible thud as the body moved inside.

"Please don't let him come out and fall on me!" Tenger shouted. He huffed and moved backward. Tenger closed his eyes, took in a deep breath, and waited for the questionable impact. The coffin plopped down with a clunk onto the ground above. Tenger exhaled. The men stared at it. "Hello?" Tenger yelled. "Toss me the rope!"

Ganter untied the coffin and threw that side of the rope to Tenger. Revie moved the horse forward and brought Tenger up out of the grave. He untied himself and threw the rope down. Kasde came to the coffin and kicked it, swearing under his breath.

Kyle grabbed the box lid and started popping out nails. The smell of rotting flesh assaulted them. Kyle was disgusted, and relieved, that the body was in there. The men helped him pull off the top. Remid brough over the meat wrapper. He handed it to Kyle. "I'm not touching him!" He cried.

Kyle stared at it for a moment. He glared at Remid and took it from his hands.

Ganter came forward. "No. I'll do it." He said. "I killed him."

Kyle shrugged and let Ganter be the one to touch the body. Ganter jostled Movada harshly, as he rolled him back and forth, to cover him with the cloth. He shoved the rope under him as he did so. Ganter breathed deeply as he maneuvered. He tied the rope in a firm knot as he finished. Ganter moved away from the body to breathe fresh air.

No one wanted to move him. No one moved. Kyle popped his neck and moved toward Movada. Tenger came to assist. The body squished and oozed fluids as they lifted. Both men gagged, but persisted. They moved swiftly together to hoist the body from the coffin, and place it, none too carefully, on the sled. Remid tied it down. Revie grabbed the reins to take the horse back to the front of the castle.

The stable boys shoved the casket back into the hole and recovered it. Kyle and Tenger ran to the trough. They needed to wash their hands from the spilt body fluids. Revie stood to the side of the castle, by the gate. "Are you going to tell us what the hell this was about?"

"We have to resurrect him to kill his soul." Kasde said in an unceremonious tone.

Remid went pale. "How exactly are you going to do that?" Revie asked, walking toward them.

Kyle looked at him. "It's complicated." He said.

Revie looked at him, and crossed his arms across his chest. "Well, uncomplicate it."

"I bought the poison from an old crone." Ganter started. "She didn't tell me that it would only kill a normal man."

Remid creased his eyebrows. "What do you mean by normal?" He asked. Revie nodded.

"We all know that this old bastard had some kind of witchcraft that he was using." Ganter replied. "He took on the form of the duke! He convinced everyone that he was Balcor! I didn't know if it made a difference!" Ganter defended.

"Well, apparently it did." Remid said.

"His demonic spirit has been taunting us." Kasde informed them. He looked at the ground. "This demon came into my bed and raped my wife! With me next to her!" Kasde shouted, angrily.

The men looked at each other. They had heard about the laughter and the mocking voices. They remained quiet.

"We visited the old crone and informed her of his doings." Tenger stated.

"She then informed me that I only asked to kill the body of a man, not of a magical being." Ganter breathed, defeatedly.

"It also turns out that she's my mother-in-law's mother!" Kyle added.

The men were shocked. Their eyes were wide with disbelief and held their mouths agape.

Remid whistled at the same time that Revie said "Damn."

"I have sent everyone away from the castle. The people need to be safe from this. My wife's family is involved in witchcraft! I have set up training in the gardens. We are going to get his soul back to his body and then kill him again! For good." Kyle told them.

"I'm coming with you." Revie stated.

"Me too." Remid nodded.

"I don't need casualties on my conscience." Kyle answered.

"No way we are staying behind." Remid said. "You need backup in a big way." He shook his head and moved closer to Kyle. "You are the king. You are our friend, and we are coming to help."

Kyle sighed. Kasde nodded his head. "We need all the help we can get. This monster has been here as well."

"Fine." Kyle moved his hands into the air. He shook his head. "We will leave as soon as Eleana gets back with the stuff she needs from the forest."

Revie and Remid looked at each other and then looked to Kyle. "Who's Eleana?"

Kyle laughed. "My witchy, grandmother-in-law."

Eleana let Ablom lead her into the forest. She knew where to go. Ablom headed for the water source, where Robbie had stopped. It was perfect. Elana needed to gather frog legs and fish eyes, as well as the tail of a squirrel. She could have gathered them from the villages, but the magic worked better if these things were fresh, and from the enchanted forest.

They could not afford to mess up, or half half-baked, sloppy potions.

Ablom was allowed to drink and roam freely. Eleana speared a fish and a frog right away. She placed the bodies into a large water container, with the water from the river, to keep it cold. The river was clear and refreshing. She breathed in the clean, fresh air. This was home. Eleana sighed. She had not been on this side of the forest in a very long time. It was different now that the fairies had gone. It was still peaceful, nonetheless.

A squirrel caught her eye. She held perfectly still. Eleana breathed out slowly. She let the forest work with her magic and slowed time. She didn't want to kill anything that she didn't have to. This was for her daughter. The squirrel jumped from one tree to the next. It went to leap into the tree next to her. Eleana caught it by the tail. She spun it around and bashed its head on a rock. The blood poured out from its tiny head.

Eleana threw the squirrel in a cloth sack, and tied it to the horse with the other things that she needed. She washed her hands in the river, and took a long drink from its coursing flow. Eleana sat on the bank for a while. She meditated on if she needed to gather anything else while she was this far. She expanded her thoughts as she refilled the magic from this place.

Fully sated, she gathered the reins of the horse, and swung up and over her. They would ride through sunset and stay the night at Vole Tirfs. Eleana hoped that they had prepared a meal. Her stomach growled as she rode. The sunset was to her side. It sent shooting colors through the sky. Orange, purple and pink could be seen from every direction. There were clouds rolling in. Eleana pushed Ablom to go faster.

Eleana was greeted by Revie and Remid at the gate. She also noticed the sled that has straw covering sack cloth. She raised an eyebrow at the men as the stench filled her nostrils.

"Ma'am" Revie greeted her. "I can take your horse to the stables. I am Revie. This is Remid. We are servants here, and we've been expecting you." He nodded to her offered her his hand to get down.

"Thank you." She obliged. "Don't touch my satchel." She instructed as Revie led the horse away.

Remid offered his elbow and walked her to the castle door. Another servant took her to a room where she could stay the night. "Do ye require anything?" The servant asked.

Eleana took a deep breath, glad to be halfway done with their journey. "I wouldn't mind some supper, if you have it." She answered.

The servant nodded her head and disappeared. She returned a few minutes later with a meal. Venison, corn and potatoes were neatly arranged on a plate. A glass of milk and a piece of bread were accompanied by a confection on the dinner tray.

"Thank you." Eleana said. "I'm famished." She sat on the edge of the bed and ate ravenously. The servant girl came and retrieved the tray as soon as she was finished. She offered her a night cap that Eleana politely refused. She stretched and laid down on the bed. No sooner than her head hit the pillow she was fast asleep.

The following morning the cock crowed that it was time to rise. Kyle opened his eyes. He had had a few too many hits from the bottle the night before. This was going to be a trying few days. Dragging the body of an enemy was one thing. Taking him to his resurrection was another. Kyle tried not to think about it as he dressed.

Kyle went downstairs and entered the dining hall. The aroma of fresh coffee and confections were delightful. Sariah was already at the table, reading a book. "Good morning." He greeted her.

"Good morning, nephew. How was your rest?" She asked.

"It was good." He lied. "How are you getting on, without your husband?" Kyle asked her.

She smiled in response. "I am fully capable of running things while he is away." She sat forward and placed her book open, face down, on the table.

"I didn't mean it as an insult to your talents." Kyle laughed. She raised her eyebrows at him and shook her brown curls. Sariah took a sip of her hot coffee and offered him a glass. He gratefully accepted.

Eleana waltzed in and joined them. She helped herself to a glass and poured some coffee into her cup. Sariah looked at her and then at Kyle.

"Sariah, this is Eleana. Robbie's grandmother." He explained. He turned to Eleana. "This is Sariah, Duchess of Vole Tirfs." He told her.

"Pardon my manners. I have a bit on my mind this morning," Eleana began. She looked around the table for sugar and cream. Sariah pushed it in her direction.

"You are pardoned." She said. Sariah smiled at her. "Welcome to our home."

"Pleased." Eleana replied sarcastically. She tossed two lumps of sugar into her cup and poured the cream in after she had stirred it in. Eleana took a gulp of the coffee and tilted her head back. "Mmmm." She breathed. "I haven't had fresh, ground coffee in a very long time." She admitted.

Sariah laughed. "Please, help yourself. I'll have the kitchen staff make some more." She rang a dinner bell. The servant girl from the night before came rushing in.

"Ma'am?" She asked.

"More coffee please. And bring out some breakfast for our guests." Sariah smiled at her and fluttered her long eye lashes.

"Right away." She nodded and disappeared.

Soon the entire traveling party was in the dining hall. They ate as if it were the only meal that they would get. Nerves were getting the best of them. Kyle introduced Tenger to his aunt. Remid and Revie told her of their plans to assist the king. Sariah welcomed Ganter back home, and informed them all that everyone was welcome to return, as they pleased.

Kyle thanked her for being such a gracious hostess. He had a larger task at hand and they needed to be moving along. Revie and Remid had packed a few things for their trip and readied the horses. Sariah had the kitchen staff make sack lunches for them, and sent them with fresh water in their canteens.

The ride back would be longer, and slower. They all had a lot on their minds. They couldn't go very fast because of the bumps in the road. They need to make sure that their smelly cargo doesn't come undone.

Kyle rode in front with Eleana, and Kasde. Tenger pulled the sled. Ganter was to his side with Revie and Remid at the rear. They wore bandanas to cover their noses. They needed to breathe, but not dust. They also didn't want to smell the corpse.

The trip was mostly silent, except for the footsteps of the horses. Some of the merchants smiled and waved hello. Kyle nodded to them and kept going. If they didn't make any stops, they would reach the castle by nightfall. They were all pushed to their limits. Tired and sore, they rode on.

The closer that they got to the castle they heard different noises. Clashes and bangs along with explosions. They also got a light show. It was easy to see in the dark. They were getting funny; questioning looks from the villagers as they passed by. The merchants were packing up their stations. The sun was setting once again. Ganter chose to make a stop. "I'll see you all in the morning." He said as he galloped away.

They finally reached the castle gates. Kyle dismounted and helped Eleana down. He took their horses to the stables. Tenger gave him a side glance as he walked away. "Um, what do you want to do with….. your cargo?" He asked.

Kyle chuckled as if he had forgotten. "Eleana?" He asked. "Do you have an answer for this question?"

She smiled back at him. "It's your place." She told him, shrugging. She continued to walk to the doorway.

Kyle sighed. "Just put it by the compost pile." He smirked. "At least then we won't notice the smell."

Tenger laughed. He moved his horse in that direction. He untied the horse from the sled and let it drop. It slid a little bit toward the pile. Tenger shrugged and walked the horse back to the stable. Kyle was brushing the horses down. He gave them grain and water. Tenger helped him where he could, carrying buckets and taking saddles and bits back to their hooks.

The men went into the castle together. Robbie ran and hugged her husband, welcoming him home. She pushed herself back from him. "Whoo, you need a bath!" She exclaimed, laughing. Robbie ordered the tub upstairs be filled with hot water. The servant obeyed, hastily. Robbie also asked that a bath be prepared downstairs for the other inhabitants, and more upstairs for her grandmother and father. They had been riding for three days.

Kyle asked that a meal be brought to him, as he relaxed in his bath. The men gathered at the dining table, awaiting refreshment and food. Clairance came down to dine with her husband, and mother. Robbie passed her going upstairs to her husband. Clairance winked at Robbie, her footsteps never faltered.

Eleana took the satchel from her hips. She handed it to the servant girl, when she finished placing the food on the table. "Place this entire thing in a cool dark place. Do not open it. Do not touch what is inside." She instructed.

The girl nodded and took the bag. Her ponytail bobbed as she walked away. She placed the satchel with the other things that Eleana had gathered before she left. They ate their food, then cleaned up as best as they could. The small number of staff able to boil water, tried to keep up with them all.

They still had the crowd outside in the tents, as well. They had eaten earlier in the day, but still required attention. People were usually easy to care for. The messes were generally about the same. Magical messes were a little more complicated. Clairance had most of it handled. Charred branches and magical ash were not something that the staff was used to dealing with.

Eleana retired for the night accepting her nightcap. Her muscles ached from riding Ablom. She had not been out this much since before she had her cave. A good night's rest was severely needed. The men slept in the servants' quarters. Clairance and Kasde ascended the stairs moments later. Balcor was sitting on the edge of his bed staring at the blade that he was toying with between his fingers.

It had been days trying to get the supernatural blade to come to life with no avail. He was exhausted. Eleana had entrusted it to him long ago. Maybe he should've figured it out then. Maybe it only came to life when it was needed, or sensed danger from another entity. Balcor had tried different hand gestures. He held it at different angles. He spun it around and fidgeted with the stones. Balcor was at a loss. He also accepted his nightcap and went to sleep. The blade rested on the bed stand next to him.

Kyle ate his dinner ravenously while he soaked in the tub. Robbie was rubbing Kyle's muscles. She used lavender oils and had placed chamomile in his bath. Kyle was not so sore from the trip, as his mind was at getting the body of a monster. He allowed his wife to massage him anyway. He reveled in her touch. The oils and scent of the bath were relaxing. Her touch was exciting his arousal. He moaned audibly. Robbie smiled. "I missed you." She whispered in his ear.

Kyle smiled back. "I've missed you too." He replied, quietly leaning his head back into her. Robbie kissed his wet tendrils. She massaged his shoulders and leaned down to rub on his muscular chest. She removed the dishes and set them to the side. She breathed in his scent deeply. Kyle moaned and began to rub her arms that were around him. He kept his eyes closed as he imagined Robbie's naked body.

He pushed her sleeves up her arms to access more flesh. "Kyle! You will ruin my gown!" She tried to pull back. Kyle moved her more forcefully against his chest and brought her around to face him. He pulled her head down and kissed her hard on the mouth. He deepened their kiss as he thrust his tongue into her mouth. She tried to move back. He stood and went with her.

Kyle walked Robbie backward to the bed. His fingers undone her gown as they moved. He backed her all the way against the bed frame. Her gown fell to the floor. He kicked it to the side. Kyle pushed Robbie backwards onto the bed. He went to his knees and held her legs apart with his powerful arms. He kissed the insides of her thighs and moved his mouth further down and in. He started licking at her sweet nub.

"Kyle! What the?" Robbie started to object. She tried to move away but he pulled her pussy into his mouth. This kind of thing was unheard of. "Oh my God!" She moaned and writhed beneath him. He licked at her pussy and clitoris. She had never experienced such sensations as were pulsing through her body. She moaned again as she sent a liquid rush to him. Kyle lapped at it and sent his tongue into her core. He sucked at her sweet juices. His tongue was working its magic within her. Her body trembled and shook in ecstasy. He was touching places that she hadn't known existed.

Kyle's tongue went back to flicking her tiny nub. He rubbed her labia with his fingers and then pushed one inside of her. He moved his finger in tune with his tongue, sending pulsing waves of vibrations inside of Robbie's entire body. Her core sent him more moisture to continue. He inserted another finger. He stretched her in circles as he licked and sucked. He pushed his hand harder into her. He began to fuck her with his fingers.

Robbie jerked back. Kyle followed her getting more onto the bed. He held her down with his arm on her stomach. He still lapped and licked at her pussy with his tongue. Robbie moaned again.

Kyle moved on top of her. He kissed up her body until he came to her breasts. He placed the entire areola into his mouth. He flicked it with his tongue as he sucked on it. He smiled into her eyes as he moved to the other side. Kyle sucked the same way on the other side. He massaged her breast with his hand, and played with the other with his tongue. Her nipples stood erect and tightened. Kyle played with the nubs with his teeth. He brought his body further upon hers.

He kissed her on the mouth again. It made his cock harder that she was tasting herself on his lips. He moved his arms down under her thighs. Kyle pushed her legs up high. He thrust himself into her. Further and further until it couldn't anymore.

Robbie tried to scream out but Kyle stopped her sounds with his kiss. She moaned into his mouth as he gave her every inch of him that her body would allow. He beat her cervix like a drum with his head. Robbie was between pain and pleasure before she exploded cum all around him. Kyle moaned as she climaxed. His cock grew more engorged. He pumped her faster and came in her wetness. She came again as he grew inside of her and sent his release with hers.

"Oh my God!" She whispered again. She lay her head down on the soft pillow. Kyle threw her a towel. "What was that?" She asked.

Kyle chuckled. "Us," he said. He wiped himself off and climbed in bed. He moved the sheets around their naked bodies. He then wrapped his arms around her. He breathed in the scent of her hair and kissed her back before falling asleep. Robbie sighed and let her hands rest between her thighs. This had made her excited, and sore. She was still pulsating from the experience, but she would never forget it.

The next morning, the sun rose casting brilliant colors through the window. The room turned pink and then orange. Robbie opened her eyes when she heard the birds singing their beautiful songs. She watched the sunrise. The arms around her gave her a feeling of peace and protection. She unconsciously played with the hair in Kyle's arm.

He smiled into her back and kissed it where his head lay. "Good morning, beautiful." He breathed.

Robbie smiled. "Good morning lover." She chuckled softly. She turned to face him. Robbie kissed his lips as they came visible. She moved downward to engage them fully. The previous night's adventure perked her mind. Her nipples became taut against his chest. Her breathing was erratic. Kyle smiled and raised his eyebrows at her. Robbie blushed.

Kyle's smile broadened. "Did you enjoy yourself last night?" he asked.

Robbie breathed deeply. She didn't want him to know how much. He already knew the answer. "You are a devil." She said. "Where on Earth did you learn these things?" She asked him, sitting up.

Kyle laughed. "I have heard a few things." He told her. "I have been at the castle a long time. I have also been a stable hand. Servants go to the stables when they want to be alone." He explained. "I have wanted to try it for a while." He smiled and winked at her.

"I had no idea your thoughts were so wicked!" She teased. "You have always been a proper gentleman." She blushed again. "Until last night."

Kyle laughed again. "We're married. What harm can it do?" He captured her mouth with his. He kissed her passionately, making her moan into his mouth. "Would you like to try it again?" He teased her by moving his hand between her thighs.

Robbie moved away. "No!" She exclaimed. "It is day!"

Kyle laughed. He sat all the way up and moved to the urinal pot. His cock was still hard from this morning's thoughts. He made

133

no move to try and hide it from her. Robbie watched him inquisitively. She licked her lips as she studied him. She couldn't believe the effect that he had on all of her senses.

Robbie silently scolded herself for being so wanton. She pretended to not be aroused. She moved to where her gown has been carelessly tossed the previous night. It was wrinkled and dirty. The sleeves were wet. She picked it up and laid it on the bed for the maids to attend to. She walked to the closet to find another. Robbie slipped on a corset and began to tie the laces.

"Would you like some help with that?" Kyle had walked silently behind her.

Robbie jumped. "I've got it. Thanks." She replied. Her nerves were on edge. She needed to find a way to calm down. His nearness wasn't helping. She could not have him touch her right now. Robbie turned to face him. "How did you get over here so fast? And quietly?" She asked. Then she exclaimed "You scared me!"

Kyle laughed at her again. "I guess I'm full of surprises." He kissed her on the forehead and walked away to dress himself.

The aroma from the kitchen wafted up to them. Robbie's stomach growled. She hurriedly finished donning her clean gown, and laced her sandals. "I'm starving." She told Kyle. "Are you ready to face the day?"

Kyle frowned and sighed. "I am as ready as I will get, love." He frowned as he remembered the task at hand. "I'd rather stay up here with you." He teased licking his lips.

Robbie laughed and tossed a pillow at his head. Kyle caught it and smiled roguishly. "Let's go before I change my mind." He whispered to her seductively. Robbie blushed and headed for the door.

CHAPTER TWELVE

The servants were scrambling to get everything ready for their guests. The dining hall was noisy as the breakfast settings were being placed. "Madam. Your Highness." The servant bobbed her head and curtsied. "What may I bring ye this day?"

Robbie smiled and nodded to her. "Coffee. Strong coffee." She said. Robbie sat at the right, to the head of the table. Kyle sat at the forefront. It was tradition.

"My lord?" Her eyes shined brightly at him. "What do ye wish?"

Kyle thought for a moment. "Milk. Crackers and honey."

The small girl bobbed her head and curtsied again. "As ye wish." She hurriedly sauntered into the kitchen.

Robbie sighed. She smiled at her husband, who just grabbed her hand to hold on the table. He caressed her skin with his fingers. Robbie stared at it.

Clairance, Kasde, and Eleana joined them shortly after. Robbie was glad for a distraction. "Mother, father, grandmother. How was your sleep?" Robbie asked them.

Eleana's blue eyes glanced from the table to Robbie and answered. "Not as good as yours." She teased her.

Robbie blushed and her mouth fell open.

"Not at the table, mother." Clairance reproved. She glared at her for a moment. Kasde laughed and shook his head.

Kyle smiled at them all. He was trying to be in a good mood for the day ahead. He nodded "thanks" to the girl as she placed his breakfast, and then Robbie's. "What news?" he asked them. "Have we everything that we need?" His brows furrowed.

Eleana nodded. "Aye."

"Are the students ready?" Kyle asked Clairance.

She thought silently before speaking. "This is a delicate task. It needs to be done quickly and efficiently." Eleana nodded and looked them each in the eyes. "We can allow him no time to get used to his body. He cannot gather his powers. I do not know how all of this will work out. The students have been working very hard. They are a talented group. We have come up with a plan." She answered.

"I hope that it doesn't involve this damned thing!" Balcor seethed, coming into the room. He placed the blade on the table. "I have tried everything."

Eleana glared at him. "You must not be so careless!" She scolded. Eleana walked to the blade and wrapped it in her napkin. She handled it like a babe. "I entrusted this to you a long time ago. I thought you would know how to use it by now!" She shouted at him.

"Old woman! Don't scold me! You never said a word, only that it would be needed in a later day!" Balcor yelled back.

"We mustn't be at war amongst ourselves!" Kyle stood raising a hand toward each of them. "We will figure it out together, uncle. Please do not fight at my table." Kyle reprimanded them.

Eleana glared at Balcor as she sat. "Old woman," Eleana sent a shock of electricity to Balcor's chair as he sat. "I'll show you old woman." She muttered under her breath as he screamed from the shock.

It was enough voltage to shock and awe, not cause pain. Balcor took his seat and scowled at her. He growled low in his chest. Balcor inhaled deeply, calming himself.

Kasde stared at them, moving his eyes from one to the other. "Well then. If that is all, let's eat." He laughed awkwardly. Oatmeal and toast were placed before them with a glass of fresh milk. Cut berries and fruit were also placed on the table, on a platter. They nodded their appreciation to the staff and ate heartily. They did not speak to one another, as they were all lost in their own thoughts. Sounds from the kitchen could be heard as they brought dishes in from the tents. Revie, Remid, and Ganter joined the table. They were laughing at something that was said before they entered the room.

"At least the men are in jovial spirits." Clairance spoke first.

"Good morning, all." Ganter said as he sat next to Balcor. Raised eyebrows and nods were all that they received from the greeting.

Ganter turned to Revie and Remid. "Looks as if we have interrupted the meeting too late." He half smirked, half grimaced.

Revie and Remid laughed. The servant brought in their breakfast. Her eyes were glued to Remid and she smiled. She curtsied and left the room.

"Well now." Revie said. "Someone has an admirer." He teased.

"Apparently several, as of late.' He nodded and he laughed.

Robbie chuckled at their banter. "Should my friends be informed?" She teased them. She gave him a mock, serious look.

Remid chuckled. "No, my lady. I have not chosen a spouse." He shook his head as if it were preposterous.

Robbie rolled her eyes at him. She grazed on a piece of an apple. The juice spurted from it, as she bit into it, landing on Kyle's nose. He looked at her and laughed before wiping it away with his napkin.

The remainder of the meal was pleasant enough. The day however would be trivial. "I believe that we should tie up the dead body before we make it live." Clairance started with her plan.

Kyle nodded. "Yes, on the rack." He makes a sound and I will stretch him until he is in pieces.

Clairance nodded. "Good. Good." She looked at Balcor. "You need to take the blade and use it, as soon as you know that he is whole." She turned to Robbie. "We will place crystals and stone to draw power from, around the grounds."

Kyle looked at Eleana. "Do you know your spell, and have your ingredients?"

She nodded. "Aye. But I will need a cooking pot and a clear area." Eleana looked at Balcor. "You will need to try again. The blade will not make itself come out enough to slay him." She rose from the table and went to find her things.

Revie and Remid were instructed to build a fire, and place a cauldron on a spit. They nodded, swallowing the rest of their food. Ganter would stand next to Tinsa and feed her energy. Tenger would do the same for Nelame. Kat would make everything appear differently than it was. Movada would not guess what was happening, until it was too late.

William and John would assist anywhere that they were needed. Kat would change the scenery. William would make a mirage. John would make him believe it.

Kyle and a few men took the sled from the hay and forged its way to the rack. Robbie assisted to heal where the body had decomposed. It needed to be whole for this to work. Clairance helped Robbie force magic into this vile man. They unwrapped him carefully, taking steps back and forth from the stench. Kyle readied the rack.

Once the body was healed, they tied his arms, legs, and neck in position. Kyle did not want to raise Movada to stretch, until he was in his body. He wanted him to feel it.

Eleana was tossing this and that into the cauldron. She mumbled her chants under her breath, circling the pot. Villae came to assist her. They chanted together. Colored smoke rose from the fire. Blue and red ash landed on the ground around them. Eleana rotated her neck and popped her bones. She spun a circle and threw in the animal pieces.

Villae reached for the sky. A magical whirlwind came from the clouds to mix the potion together. Eleana raised her arms as well and made the tornado bigger. Clairance and Robbie joined them. Dirt and debris flew around the castle. The clouds darkened and lightning struck the pot. The women continued. They circled the fire pit with their eyes closed, and joined hands.

Villae craned her neck and began shaking. She was muttering something incomprehensible. Her bones cracked and she fell. Eleana shouted "Keep going!" over the storm before them. Robbie started to shake as the cauldron did. Tinsa sent her power through her fingers. Kat added hers to Clairance. They steadied one another as they had trained to do.

The men watched fascinated. They were also slightly scared and mortified. William and the fairies came to assist. They dragged Villae from the circle. She was dead. The fairies started to weep. Their tears were picked up by the storm and blew into the potion. The pot exploded! Robbie and Clairance practically landed on top of one another. Eleana was blown back. She sat straight up and conjured a vile to catch the elixir. It was done.

The women stay on the ground panting. Fairies came to Villae's body and covered her in flowers. Eleana, Clairance, and Kasde cried. Robbie struggled to regain her breath. She panted heavily. Her stomach lurched, and then she threw up next to her. Tinsa gasped. "Robbie! Are you ok?"

Robbie wiped her mouth with her arm and sniffled. She swallowed the taste in her mouth before she answered. "I am fine."

Tinsa helped her to her feet. They in turn helped up the others. Villae's body could be dealt with later. They had more important business to attend to. The potion needed to be used while it was fresh. Eleana went to the rack.

Kat changed the scenery. It looked as if Movada was sitting in his throne room. William conjured Sydney to sit on his lap. John held his temples, forcing the image to be correct in Movada's mind. He wouldn't feel the ropes until it was too late. The rest of them scattered next to the rocks that were placed. They pooled the energy from the crystals into their bodies.

Clairance and Robbie joined hands. Kyle was at the rack's mechanical device. Revie and Remid readied their swords. Eleana handed the blade back to Balcor. Ganter stood behind Tinsa to steady her, and feed her energy. Nelame and Tenger did the same from a crystal on the other side.

Dark clouds formed around them. The magic in their air grew thick. The eyes of the witches began to glow. Eleana opened Movada's mouth and poured the vile into it. Robbie and Clairance made him swallow. Eleana started her spell.

"Corpus et anima reunite, sana mortuis. Intrare daemonium! Ad hoc corpus vitam faciunt!" Eleana chanted the words and sent her magic into him. The witches joined by pointing their hands in her direction. Magic flowed from all around into Eleana. From Eleana it went into Movada. His body started to rise. The healing spell worked from Clairance and Robbie. His mouth opened and shut. He swallowed more of the potion. His fingers clenched and opened. Movada's eyes flew open to see Eleana pushing magic into him.

"Woman! What have you done?" He growled at her.

Eleana began anew. "Now!" She told the others. Kyle stretched Movada's body tight. "Totum occidere! Corpus et anima." Eleana shouted over Movada's screams. The witches sent her more power. She repeated her spell. Balcor found the strength to withhold the blade. The dagger's point grew longer. Movada tried to get loose. He could not tell what had him bound. He saw the throne room. He began to raise his hand to stop the magic around him.

Balcor moved forward swiftly. He rammed the blade through Movada's heart. The rack pulled his body to pieces. "God, send his soul back to Hell!" Balcor yelled. Eleana continued to chant. The powers ran through them all. Movada's body was dead and the demon came for them.

"Daemonium mittat in gehannam!" Eleana yelled with all of the power from the grounds. The demon writhed and made awful noises that could not be described. It floated up and burst into flames.

Tinsa sent more power to the fire. Kat brought more heat. The demon and the body parts squealed and turned to ash. Nelame sent a water current to it. Eleana conjured a container for the remains.

Robbie fed her strength to her grandmother. Clairance pushed hers into her as well. Kasde fed them both more. The fairies came in and helped push all of the dust and soot from the demon into the container. Movada was gone. His soul had been incinerated. Nelame and Tinsa washed the entire thing clean. They moved the crystals around the remains and covered the jar with salt. All was done and over.

The women and men fell to the ground as thunder shook the area. Kyle blew out a sigh of relief as the clouds passed by. John willed them to go back to normal. The women lay still on the ground, drained. Revie and Remid checked to make sure they were breathing.

Robbie tried to sit up. Her head was spinning. Her stomach lurched again. She tried to keep it down. There was nothing left for her to empty from her gut. She dry-heaved a few more times. Robbie took slow deep breaths to steady her body. She sat still until the dizziness left her.

Balcor helped the women sit up. Then men took them one by one into the castle. The staff prepared hot drinks for them with a shot of alcohol. "Tea, please." Robbie asked faintly. The servant nodded and ran to fetch it.

People were resting around the guest entrance. Each one regaining the strength to stand and speak. Movada was powerful. Defeating him, body and soul, had drained everyone. Peace could now be a more permanent fixture in the kingdom. With the power of Eleana and her family plus the energy from the villagers, it was done.

Kyle inhaled a deep breath and let out a sigh of relief. The family was safe and back inside. With the ritualistic slaughter over, he could have the staff come back and resume things as they should be. He heard Robbie gasp. "Are you ok?" He asked her.

She glanced at him and swallowed a burp. "I fear my coffee may have upset my stomach." She told him. Her stomach lurched again. "Do we have any soda crackers?" She placed her hand at her throat.

Kyle looked at her with concern showing on his face. "I will find out." He ran off to the kitchen.

The servant came back sooner than Kyle did, with her tea and crackers. Clairance moved closer to Robbie. "What's the matter dear?" Clairance moved Robbie's hair behind her ear, and placed her hand on Robbie's forehead. She smiled at her daughter. "You are not ill." She told her.

Robbie cocked her head at her mother. "No. I am not ill; I just have an upset stomach." She spoke.

Clairance grabbed Robbie's hand and patted it. She sent healing energy to her. She felt the presence of another. She had been envisioning a child for a while now. She hadn't gotten the vision of whom it would be from. "Robbie! You're pregnant!"

Robbie's face paled. "No, I am not." She replied.

Clairance giggled and smiled wider. Kyle returned with more crackers. Clairance smiled at him. She looked at him with fondness. "Kyle." She stated. She looked him in the eye. "You are going to need more than crackers." She chuckled again leaving her daughter's side.

Kyle sat where Clairance had just retreated. "What was that about?" He asked Robbie.

Robbie sighed and sipped her tea. She looked at her husband and then ate a cracker to settle her stomach.

"Robbie?" Kyle asked her again.

Robbie licked her lips. She looked Kyle in the eye. "It's preposterous!" She laughed and looked away.

"What is?"

She laughed again. "Mother thinks that I am pregnant." Her eyes widened as she told him. She smiled slightly and then rolled her eyes.

Kyle sat forward. He placed his head in his hands. "Well." Was all he said. He frowned and then he smiled. "We are having a baby?" He asked again, in shock from the news. He looked at Clairance. "Are you sure?" He asked her. His eyes were wide. Clairance smiled in return and shrugged her shoulders.

Kyle sat next to his wife and took one of her crackers. He was also now feeling under the weather. He looked from Robbie's face to her stomach, and then back again. Kyle shook his head and smiled. He kissed Robbie on the forehead and held her hand.

Since Villae's death, the magic in the kingdom was fading. The fairies were dispersing one by one. Eleana moved her things with a flip of her wrist, into the cottage where Clairance had raised Robbie. She sat at the kitchen table and laughed. Eleana secretly knew that when one life of power expels, another begins. Their child would be the heir to the kingdom, the heir to the magic, and powerful.

The end....

For now...

www.ingramcontent.com/pod-product-compliance
Lightning Source LLC
Chambersburg PA
CBHW060331260626
47160CB00007B/2765